THE
UMBRAS

Derek E. Keeling

THE
UMBRAS

Derek E. Keeling

Dare Ric Media

A division of SouthEast Productions

Portland, Oregon 97202

Published by
Dare Ric Media
a division of
SouthEast Productions
Portland, Oregon 97202

Copyright © 2011 Derek E. Keeling

First Edition 2011

All rights reserved. No part of this book may be reproduced, stored in a retrieval system, or transmitted, in any form or by any means, electronic, mechanical, photocopying, recording or otherwise, without the prior permission of the author and/or publisher, except in the case of brief quotations embodied in critical articles and reviews, or where permitted by law.

This is a work of fiction. Names, characters, places, and incidents are either the product of the authors imagination or are used fictitiously. Any resemblance to actual persons, living or dead, events, or locales is entirely coincidental.

Photography Copyright © 2011 Shad Hamilton
Cover Artwork Copyright © 2011 Travis Sims

ISBN   978-1-257-76278-1

Author Email: dareric1@yahoo.com
Author Blog: http://derekkeeling.blogspot.com

Printed in the United States of America by Lulu

10   9   8   7   6   5   4   3   2   1

For my Mother, Father, Brother, and Grandparents. ***Ego Diligo Vos***

Contents

Chapter One……………………1
Chapter Two………………....17
Chapter Three………………33
Chapter Four……………...51
Chapter Five…………………69
Chapter Six………………..89
Chapter Seven……………...101
Chapter Eight…………….119
Chapter Nine……………….135
Chapter Ten………………...151
Chapter Eleven…………….169

Chapter 1
On The Case

Derek E. Keeling | 2

The Umbras

The Umbras

He knew just by looking through the hazy, amber colored glass window that someone was standing outside his office door. The window hung dead center in the middle of the poorly painted white door displaying the words, Private Detective Walter Pierce. He had stared at these words for years, always looking at them backwards; it had begun to drive him nuts. But this time he stared through the words at the silhouette of a woman. He could see her head moving back and forth and her hands coming up and touching her face. His eyes grew with curiosity at the unknown beauty at his doorstep. Yet she made no effort to knock or say anything to let him know of her presence. His patience was wearing thin.

He stood from his old oak desk chair as silently as he could, but the chair moaned and creaked with a violent furiousness. The silhouette in the window jumped and threw her hands to her face but did not leave, or, for that matter, inquire with a knock. She stood there, silent, but not motionless. As he walked from behind his desk to his office door, the floor screamed a thousand screams. The sound was slightly reminiscent of camping in a heavily wooded area during a windstorm. It gave him no such luck in the area of stealth. His hand grasped the door handle tightly; he caught a beautiful whiff of women's perfume. He drew it in deep, allowing the wonderful lavender and rose fragrance to permeate within his soul. The door rattled as it swung open and finally came to a rest against the wall, slamming just enough to frighten the woman.

"Oh, you scared me," she gasped placing her hand over her chest.

"I apologize; I didn't mean to startle you," he replied. "Is there something I can help you with? I've noticed you've been standing outside my door for a few minutes." As these words came out of his mouth, he realized the woman was crying. Two thick lines of washed away makeup told the story. The woman was in a beautiful red dress that clung tightly to her frame. She carried a small black handbag with two handles at her side. Her hair was thick and blond but looked soft. It hung from her head and gently kissed her shoulders, dancing back and forth in long golden strands of angelic silk.

"Yeah, I'm sorry, I was just trying to pull myself together before I came in and talked to you." She lifted her hand up and brushed her hair back behind her ear. "I have a case for you, assuming you want it." Her eyes met with his as she said this, and he drew in a deep breath.

"Yeah, sure, come in and we can talk about it," he said exhaling and waving his hand toward the chair that sat in front of his desk. She walked into his office slowly, going straight for the chair. The heels of her shoes clicked with every step and were amplified by the room's natural reverb. She placed her handbag down on the floor as she sat in the chair.

"I guess we could start with our names. I'm Detective Walter Pierce," he stated as he stretched his hand across the desk towards her, waiting for a name and a handshake.

She brought her hand up from her lap and placed it into his. Her skin was as white as bone, yet it was as soft as the petals of a rose. She had the grip of a sophisticated gentle woman, and nails as red as the fires of hell.

"My name is Marcia Darden," she told him. "I am the wife…well, I was the wife…" Her voice became broken and filled with a genuine sadness. "Neil Darden was my husband. He was murdered about a week ago." Marcia's head sunk down below her shoulders and she let out a sob that sent a shudder down Walter's spine.

"Here, take one of these." He held out a small opened metal box containing several cigarettes. She took one and placed it upon her lips. The vibrant red lipstick smeared slightly onto the filter of the cigarette. Walter held out a lighter and lit the cigarette for her.

"Thank you very much," she said while exhaling her first drag. "You have no idea how much I needed this." Walter took a cigarette out of the box for himself and quickly lit it up, blowing smoke across the room.

"So, how did you come about needing the services of a Private Detective?" he said grinning a little trying to liven up the mood. He always hated dealing with the victim's families of the cases he worked on. They were always so sad and depressed, lacking the same amount of life as the ones they've lost, or so he thought.

Marcia's eyes wandered away from the conversation. She took a deep drag of her cigarette and stared at Walter's plaques and awards. He had a framed document stating his legality in the Private Detective business. He had awards that he had won for saving lives and committing brave acts of heroism. Smoke started to fill the small room— a thick haze in which it was hard to keep your eyes open from the burning smoke. The walls were tinged a yellow-brown from the heavy smoking habits of current and past tenants. A single metal fan pointed out a window offered the only chance of ventilation. Walter stood from his chair, opened the window and turned the fan on. It hummed like that of a thousand wasps gathering in a field of wildflowers.

"There we go. Get a little air in here," Walter mumbled as if speaking only to himself. He sat back down and looked at Marcia. "Hey, are you okay?" he asked noticing her lack of communication. She sat silently and still, staring at the plaques and awards that adorned the Detective's wall. "Hey, are you..."

"I hear you're the best," she interrupted and then paused. "I hear you'll take cases that sometimes don't make much sense, or don't have very much evidence. You know, the weird ones," Marcia blurted, never once making eye contact with Walter. "Is this true?" Her eyes shot down from the wall and stabbed into the Detective through his eyes.

"I, uh, have been known to take rather weird cases, and to have a rather weird approach at the cases I take. I have taken cases that were previously deemed solved, unsolved or closed. And after investigating further into those cases, have truly solved them. As you can tell by the plaques and awards on the wall." He said this with a little bit of smugness, and felt slightly ashamed. "But to answer your question with a little less egotism: yes. Yes I have taken cases like these."

"Your reputation around Francis City is impeccable. Your egotism is truly justified," she replied bowing in her seat with the grace and beauty and an angel. There was an awkward silence for a moment while Walter blushed and tried to regain himself.

"Before we go any further, let's talk about fees," he said.

"Yeah, sure. What's your price?" she asked.

"Well, I'm not cheap. In fact, I'm pretty expensive," he replied.

"Money is no problem." She pulled out a black checkbook and pen and began to write on a blank check.

"I charge $100 an hour. Plus, half of $5000.00 up front for expenses," he said. She started scratching even quicker across the checkbook and then ripped out the check.

"Like I said," she smiled. "Moneys no problem. That's $10,000 for you to work with. If you need more, let me know" she said proudly. Walter took the check and after looking it over, crammed it into his pocket.

"Thank you. This should suffice for now," Walter said gratefully. "So, now that that's out of the way. What happened to your husband that you would like me to investigate?" he asked curiously.

"Well, that depends on who you ask." Her eyes once again fell to the floor. "I'm sure he was murdered, murdered right in front of me." Marcia's eyes began to swell up with tears, she gritted her teeth to try and hold them back. Walter could sense the urgency, the need for justice in her voice and actions. He knew she didn't come here for fun, or to waste time. She wanted closure on something, or validation.

"Why do you think that?" Walter asked calmly. Marcia took a deep breath; her eyes shuffled around in her head looking for the right words.

"Okay, here it is." She took another breath and placed her hands on Walter's desk to fiddle around with one of his stray paper-clips. "My husband and I were sitting in our living room enjoying a nice fire. I was reading a book, and he was going over some papers that had to do with some project he had been working on for work. Anyway, we sat in silence for maybe two hours, not saying a word to each other. We just went about our own business. The only noise in the room was the occasional pop or crack from the fireplace." She paused to take it all in. "The fire had started to die down. So I went to put more wood on it. I walked over to our fireplace, which is no more than ten feet away from where we were sitting." Her voice squeaked and she stopped and took a big drag off her cigarette, which at this point was nothing but cigarette filter. The drag wafted across the room. A smelly chemical scent tickled at Walter's nostrils. He pushed a thick, metal ashtray toward Marcia. "I was standing there throwing a piece of wood on the fire when I heard a thud from behind me in Neil's direction. I looked back and he was laying face first on the floor, dead." She stopped again and smashed her cigarette against the side of the ashtray. "The weird thing is, right after I noticed Neil was on the ground, I saw a shadow," she added. She could see a slight look of doubt in Walter's eyes, which Walter did not mean to show. "A real one. I wasn't imagining things. Something moved from the living room into the kitchen, then left out of the back door," she added defensively. "I know this because the back door was unlocked and we never left it unlocked, ever. Also, all his papers were missing from the table."

"What did the police say?" Walter questioned breaking his silence.

"They think he died naturally. They said his heart just stopped. They said it was as quick as snapping a finger, that he felt no pain. Can you believe that? How insincere does one have to be to say something like that to someone whose husband just died? They closed the case the same day, no investigation, nothing. They say he just died of natural causes. But I know he was murdered. Call it hunch, call it what you will. I know." Walter studied her face as she replied. She was obviously broken up about all that had happened to her. Marcia's stiffened up as she added, "I don't know if this'll help, but. Neil was working on a project. A 'top secret' project." She put her fingers up in front of herself and signaled quotations. "This project consumed him, it's all he ever did for months. It was so secret, he wouldn't even tell me where he worked. He worked with one other person. That I do know for sure. I've seen a picture of him once but, besides that, I don't know anything about what he was doing. He wouldn't tell me about it. All he would say was that this project, once completed, would change the world forever. He was always into those weird conspiracy theories like: UFO's, Roswell, JFK. But he used to always talk about this one conspiracy. He said that if he didn't watch out that these people would 'erase' him. I didn't realize that he was serious." Her head shook back and forth with a look of disgust. There was a sense of panic in her voice, which filled the air with a thick tension. "I remember him talking about these people, these assassins. He used to say things like they would kill without anyone noticing, even the person they were killing. And they hide in the shadows. All to silence whoever gets in the way of their ideals." She paused and pushed the ashtray toward Walter. "Am I crazy?" she asked rhetorically. "I mean, does any of this make any sense, or, seem like it's worth your time? It's pretty unusual."

The Umbras

"You're not crazy, trust me. But, I've got to admit, that's a very unusual case," Walter said. He placed his hand on top of Marcia's and smiled warmly, just barely showing his teeth. "Unusual or not, I'd love to investigate it."

"Thank you," she replied, returning the smile.

"I'd like to start off by doing a little research on the case. And I'm going to need your help whenever I can get it. Do you think you can try to find that photograph, or at least try to get a name of who Neil was working with. It might help to talk with him. Plus, any paperwork or documents you can get me would be very helpful," Walter said.

"Well, I have a few documents with me actually." She reached down into her purse and pulled out a small assortment of papers. Some were typed, others were hand written. "The police and the coroner's report are on the top. The rest are kind of unknown to me." She laid the papers down in front of him with trembling hands. Walter picked up the small stack and straightened them out.

The Umbras

"I promise you, I will do everything in my power to get to the bottom of this. I am going to need a few days to get myself acquainted with the case. I am really curious to know why Detective…" Walter scanned the first paper titled: Police Report, searching for the Detective in charge. "Detective Frank Barlow…" he said raising an eyebrow. "…closed the case so quickly."

"Do you know him?" she asked, sensing his awkwardness.

"Uh…yeah. Frank and I go way back, so to speak. I've had a lot trouble with him. But I've also got a lot of help from him." Walter admitted hesitantly.

"Is he a good cop? You know, does he do his job correctly and thoroughly?" Her voice got a little louder when she said this and her nostrils flared.

"I hate to say it, but Frank has been known to be the kind of Detective that does the very least amount of work he can, pawning all the real work onto dumb street cops who don't know anything about being a Detective. This could explain the quick closure of the case." As he announced this, Marcia stood from her chair, taking her purse with her and throwing her hair from her shoulder as she walked toward the door. This wasn't what she wanted to hear. Walter was never very suave when it came to saying the right things to women. He always had a tendency to just blurt out whatever he was thinking.

"Just please do what you can. My phone number is on the police report if you need to get ahold of me," she said pointing at the stack of papers with a hint of fire in her voice. "And Detective…" She opened the door and a violent rattle emitted from the frame. "Thank you."

"I'll do everything I can," he declared as she closed the door. He could hear the clicking of her heels as she walked down the hallway toward the main exit of the building. He lit up another cigarette and drew the smoke deep into his lungs. He sat still, staring at the door. Smoke billowed up at him, stinging at his nose and eyes. He loved new cases. He loved the thrill, but most importantly, he loved the justice.

Chapter 2
Mystery In The Morgue

Derek E. Keeling | 18

The Umbras

The Umbras

Walter squinted his eyes fiercely at the perfectly cube shaped building. The rain dripped heavily off his wide-brimmed brown fedora, splashing onto the dark asphalt. The wind tore through his trench coat, sending a shudder down his back. He hated the morgue. To him it represented a place of absolute disrespect of the dead. Poking and prodding at a dead human was a little on the unusual side for him. The smell of formaldehyde and the cheap air freshener the Mortician used to mask the smell of death always made Walter sick to his stomach. A small, rectangular sign above the door read: Welcome.

"That's a little creepy," Walter whispered to himself as he turned the door handle.

As he stepped into the morgue, the smell hit him. It smelled like road kill that had been baking in the sun for a few days, then set right under your nose. His gag reflexes started to kick in, causing him to choke slightly. He quickly covered his face with his trench coat collar. The overhead light flickered around, casting shadows on the walls that appeared stained with the stench of death. The place was sad, dirty, and lacked anything to temporarily take your mind off the reason why you were here. Death, whatever the sort. "Thankfully," Walter thought, "I'm here to investigate death, not to mourn or visit it."

"Sir, can I help you with something?" a voice asked from the office to the right of Walter.

"Uh…yes, sorry. I am Private Detective Walter Pierce. I'm investigating the Darden case," Walter answered still covering his nose and displaying his credentials.

"Ah…yes, Neil Darden. Strange case, strange case," the man said shaking his head and ruffling through some papers. "Please, step into my office and we'll discuss it. I am Edward Brussels, by the way."

"It's nice to meet you Mr. Brussels. Please forgive me for being so forward, but where is Nathan?" Walter implored.

"He's on vacation. I'm not normally a mortician. They just needed someone with experience to fill in for Him while he's gone," Edward stated. "And please, call me Eddie," He added.

"What do you do, normally?" Walter asked.

"I'm a research scientist," he answered.

"Interesting work?" Walter asked

"Very much so," Eddie replied. Edward

Derek E. Keeling

The Umbras

Brussels was a tall and lengthy stick of a man. Wild red bushy eyebrows and a moustache that seemed to flicker with fiery torment at the end of each of his sentences. Freckles clung tightly to the skin of his body in uncountable quantities. His eyes hung low and sleepy with dark bags. The stress of a being mortician had obviously gotten to him. He sat awkwardly in his chair which squeaked every time he moved. "Please, come in. Take a seat."

Walter entered the office and relinquished the collar from his nose. "Do you mind if I smoke? The smell of this place really gets to me," Walter said pulling the chair from the desk and sitting in it.

"As long as you don't mind if I join you?" Eddie said. He pulled out a small, rectangular red box. A big horseshoe and a four-leaf clover adorned the front of the box, symbolizing luck. An unusual word in bold green letters at the top of the box caught Walter's attention.

"Finis?" Walter read. "Never heard of them."

"They are imported, very hard to find," Eddie said with a smear of sophistication. He pulled a cigarette from the box. Across the side of the entire cigarette was printed, in bold green, 'Finis'. A brown filter with a small diamond shaped pattern entered Eddie's mouth.

"Need a light?" Walter offered, holding his lighter toward Eddie.

"Thank you," Eddie said puffing greatly from the long cigarette. It's filter was immensely small in proportion to the rest of the cancer stick.

The lighter Walter` used to light his cigarettes was a gift given to him by his ex-wife for their one year anniversary, as was the cigarette case. It was sort of a set. Made of high polished stainless steel and engraved with his initials: W.P., he carried it with him always. Mainly because he was a regular smoker. It had nothing to do with the fact that it was a gift from his ex-wife.

The room, which was poorly lit to match the eerie quality of the morgue, was set aglow as Walter drew in a lung full of the satisfying smoke. With little results he blew the smoke out in a solid stream, moving his head back and forth trying to cover as much area with the scent as possible. Reaching across the desk, Walter flicked his cigarette, splashing ash onto neighboring papers.

"So what would you like to know about

The Umbras

Neil Darden?" Edward inquired dusting off the stray ash.

"Well, for starters, a minute ago you shook your head and said something about it being a strange case; what did you mean?" Walter answered and asked curiously.

"Um...let's see. How do I put this?" he pondered scratching his chin, which seemed to echo violently in the tiny office. "It was determined by the on-site examiner that Neil Darden died naturally. But after I checked him out, I found there to be a single injection hole at the top of his spine. Made from a very small syringe. After finding this out, I did some tests to see if maybe he was poisoned. My results were unusual at best," Edward paused and waited for some sort of recognition from Walter.

"What did it turn out to be?" Walter replied anxiously, sitting up in his chair and taking another drag from his cigarette.

"Well...That's what turned out to be unusual." he paused once more. This time pushing a piece of paper in front of Walter and tapping on what appeared to be a chart or graph. "This is something science has never seen before." His eyebrows lifted suddenly as he said this.

The Umbras

"And I take it you assume that this is what killed him?" Walter chimed.

"Well…uh?" Edward stuttered, nervously shuffling his eyes around for an answer. "Well…no. I would say…I would have to agree with the on-site examiner, based on Neil's age and health," he pleaded. At this moment Edward's skin became flush and beads of sweat were scattered about his forehead. Walter could tell Edward was lying, or at least holding something back. "It probably had something to do with that 'top secret experiment' he was working on, maybe a self-test gone wrong." Edward's eyes opened large as he realized what he had just said. A brief silence followed as Walter drew in the moment and another drag from his cigarette, which lit the room into an orange blaze.

"How did you find out about the top secret project? It doesn't seem so top secret if you know about it." Walter put simply.

"I…uh. Heard it through the grapevine. You know how these things get passed down from one person to the other. Kind of like that game, telephone," Edward rambled.

"Yeah…I know," Walter remarked looking Edward up and down in his chair. He could tell something wasn't being said. Information wasn't being released. He didn't want to press too hard with the questions. But the detective in him was clawing to get out. The tension in the room began to grow as the silence became longer.

"I'm only doing my job. I'm not the bad guy here, remember?" Edward said.

"Yeah I know. Well, if you see anything else that you think I should know about, here's my card. You can call me anytime," Walter said handing Edward a business card. Edward let out a deep sigh and glanced over the card.

"Yeah…I'll do that," He replied.

"Thank you," Walter uttered reaching his hand out toward Edward's for a shake.

"No problem," Edward said grasping Walter's hand loosely.

As Walter threw the door to the front of the Morgue open, he took a deep breath, bringing relief to the smell that he had endured inside. But the relief was temporary as he shook his trench coat and noticed the smell was deeply embedded in his clothes. "That's not coming out," he thought. The night air chilled the detective to the bone. A heavy fog had set over the dark streets, strangling away any clear view. Every twenty-five yards or so, pale streetlights beamed vibrantly at the ground, which made the streets in between that much darker. The rain had finally stopped its downpour. But it left the streets soaked. The entire night just felt weird, much like the case felt to Walter.

"Pssst...sir," a voice from behind him whispered. Walter quickly jerked his head back, placing his hand at his hip onto his pistol; a beautiful .357 Magnum that packs a loud punch. His eyes scanned the foggy abyss that surrounded him, he saw nothing. He slowly and as quietly as he could unsnapped the holster. "Over here," the voice said again. This time Walter could vaguely see a man standing in the alley adjacent to the morgue. The alley was about ten feet across, with walls that chased towards the sky with imprisoning accuracy. A single light flickered on and off and rocked back and forth gently with the wind. Garbage cans and dumpsters littered the alley. Yet most of the garbage was thrown carelessly onto the ground. Walter kept his hand on his gun as he entered the alley. He hated a lot of things: the smell of morgues, grieving families, and even spiders. But one thing he hated more was having to use his gun to take the life of another. Killing wasn't in his blood, investigating

The Umbras

was. To Walter, life was too precious to be taken away by anyone, under any circumstances. And besides, he thought it was a harsher punishment to put someone into a cell and have them reflect on their life wasted, instead of killing them and having them get off 'easy'. Walter's shoes squeaked on the wet pavement as he passed a dumpster. The sound reverberated throughout.

"What can I do for you sir?" Walter shouted at the man who was still about five or ten yards away from him.

"Please, I'm not going to harm you," the man said obviously noticing Walter's hand fixed onto his gun. "I just have some information I think that you should know." Walter cautiously withdrew his hand from his gun and came in closer to the man. He was a short man with stubby little legs. His arms waved Walter in closer, flapping each time. The man's hair was a dark brown, and laid straight down onto his ears. It shined with a greasy sheen as if it hadn't been washed in days. As Walter stepped in close enough to see the man's face he noticed his eyes bulging and his movements running amuck with fear. The man's hands trembled and ripped at his hair, trying to straighten it out, only to mess it up even worse. He wore a pair of old bloody scrubs, with the blood splatter mask pulled down around his neck, stained thoroughly.

"So what's this about?" Walter asked bringing one eyebrow up confusingly.

The man quickly looked around, as if someone was watching them in the alley talking. The man was clearly paranoid. Walter thought this was a weird night to begin with, but this was certainly beginning to finalize the deal.

"I have some information on the case you are working on," the man answered quietly still looking around suspiciously.

"Is that so. And just who are you?" Walter asked sternly.

"My name is Thomas. Thomas Webster. I am the mortician's assistant." He stated proudly.

"How come I've never seen you around here?" Walter questioned, still trying to figure out the situation at hand.

"I just started here about three weeks ago. Plus they kind of keep me out of sight." Thomas said.

"Why is that" Walter replied. Thomas gestured by pointing to his clothes. "Makes sense." Walter chuckled. "Alright…so anyways, continue."

The Umbras

"Well…About a week ago, a body comes rolling in. We were running through all the normal motions, when I found an injection hole," Thomas stated.

"Wait, so you found the injection hole?" Walter interrupted.

"Yes," he stated abruptly. "We were studying the injection mark after I found it on the victim. We were working fast to try and gather evidence. I knew the case was closed, but after finding that mark, I urged Eddie to at least do a preliminary examination. He didn't want to do it, he said we could get into a lot of trouble. But I figured something was up."

At that moment a car's headlights broke the darkness of the alley as it drove by. A breath left Thomas as he walked further into the alley, still searching for eavesdroppers. Walter was beginning to feel like he too was being watched, or listened to. His paranoia coaxed him into following Thomas. Walter stepped into the dark shadow Thomas was hiding in; he could barely see his silhouette.

"As I was saying, we knew the case was closed. So we were working fast. Eddie instructed me to go into the supply room and get a couple things for the examination. It only took me maybe like five minutes. But when I got back he was very shaken up," Thomas said.

"Why? What happened?" Walter asked.

"Eddie said someone came into the room with him. He said he was the lead investigator of the Darden Case. Apparently Eddie started telling him about the injection marks and how he had reason to believe that Neil Darden did not die naturally, but was murdered." Thomas got quiet for a moment. Walter noticed him looking around nervously.

"So he was lying to me?" Walter declared.

"He had to. They threatened his life," Thomas interjected defensively.

"Wait…Who threatened his life?" Walter asked stunned.

"The lead investigator. He told Eddie that the men died naturally and that he had to stop any further examination of the bodies. At that point he said he got very offended and started telling the lead investigator about bringing this information in front of a judge. Then the man slammed Eddie up against a wall and told him that if he didn't forget about what he'd discovered, it'd be him lying on the examination table with injection marks." Once again Thomas became silent, frozen still in the shadow of the alleyway like a mannequin.

"Then what happened?" Walter asked curiously.

"The man left. He took the film out of our camera, and took our notes. This really made Eddie mad, so he continued with the examination even with these threats. He ran all sorts of tests. Nothing really came up until he ran a toxin test. It seems that Neil Darden died from some unknown toxin injected into the top of the spine, killing him instantly."

"Have either of you told anyone about this?" Walter implored. The eeriness of the alleyway disappeared as Walter was enthralled further into Thomas's story.

"No. Eddie was going to say something about it to someone, but decided against it," Thomas answered.

"Why?" Walter prodded further.

"He didn't want to die," Thomas explained.

"So why haven't you said anything to someone?" Walter asked.

"Well, I don't want to die either. And I'm telling you aren't I? Standing in this dark alley, fearing for my life," he replied.

The Umbras

"Try not to worry so much, I doubt anyone is watching us." Walter said trying to comfort Thomas. "Is there any information you could give me on the person who threatened Edward Brussels, a name or…anything?"

"Yeah…" Thomas motioned Walter close to him and whispered, " Eddie said his name was, Detective Frank Barlow."

Chapter 3
Where It All Started

Derek E. Keeling | 34

The Umbras

Derek E. Keeling

The Umbras

The room was crowded with stale cigar smoke. It stung at Walter's eyes, which was abnormal considering his smoking habit. Angry cops and suspects littered the station filling the atmosphere with a dense effervescence of hatred, and complete and utter confusion. Conversations cluttered around each other, blending together in a harmonious symphony of anguish. Walter could make out a few words: talks of jail-time, court dates, plea bargains, and freedom. All the normal things Walter had gotten use to in the five years he spent as a cop at the Francis City Police Department. But the current scene of the station, if you didn't know what was happening, was total chaos.

The wait seemed like forever. The solid white oak bench he sat on offered no support; his cramped backside showed the evidence. As he tried to adjust himself, he thought he heard someone talking in his direction. As his head twisted sharply toward his right he caught the eyes of the receptionist, who was at that time staring into his eyes from about three feet away.

"Detective Barlow will see you now," she said with a concerning look in her eye. The kind of concerning look only a small elderly woman with vibrant, white, curly hair could give.

"Ok," Walter said standing up and following the woman. Frank Barlow's office was in the back right of the station, through a sea of desks, cops, and convicts. Every street hardened criminal of Francis City glared at Walter as he passed. "I must look like a cop," he thought. A mean looking man with scars covering his face and hands snarled at Walter. "Or maybe I smell like one," he wondered. A plaque hung sadly from the center of Frank's door: Detective Frank Barlow Lead Investigator F.C.P.D. It was the office every cop 'dreamed of'. Walter knocked briskly on the thick wood door and could faintly hear the deep raspy sound of Frank telling him to come in. It wasn't the first time he had heard Frank utter those words.

"What's this all about, Pierce?" Frank said pouring himself a drink as Walter shut the door. Frank Barlow was a drinker. There was no doubt about that. He had the look of an age hardened alcoholic bent on personal destruction. His eyes hung low and dark, shattering the kind souls of anyone daring enough to stare into them. His swollen body fit snuggly inside the unwashed brown mess of a suit he wore. A few buttons on his shirt were missing and he wore his tie loosely around his neck. He was a disaster, that was for sure. But, he was probably the only cop in the city with a good collection of expensive gin and whiskey. This much he was good for.

"May I?" Walter asked insinuating that a drink was in order.

Walter wasn't much of a drinker. But being back in this building brought on a sudden thirst for a stiff whiskey on ice.

"Help yourself, just don't make a mess," Frank replied sitting himself into his chair. Walter looked around the room sarcastically. The place was a veritable pigsty.

"I don't think I could do much damage," Walter said jokingly.

"Hey, if you got a problem with it, get the hell out," Frank snapped. "What do you want anyway? I've got a lot of work to do and it seems like once again your wasting my time."

"Actually, I was wondering about the homicide case you closed so quickly," Walter said casually. His boldness brought a sickening look over Frank's face.

"What in God's name are you talking about?" Frank asked.

"The Neil Darden case," Walter answered.

"Oh…I see. Let me guess…Marcia Darden?" Walter said bringing his drink up to his mouth and drinking heavily, spilling ice and streams of aged whiskey out the corners of his mouth and onto his suit. He stood from his chair and began to pour himself another drink, this time twice as big. The antique crystal decanter rung out vibrantly as he rattled it up against the whiskey glass. The notes the crystal produced were angelic, mesmerizing, a sonata of light cascading across a tidal wave of sound that finally comes together between an ocean of ice and spirits. His glass was half-full, but the expression frozen on his face suggested that it was indeed, half-empty.

"Yes. It was Marcia that brought this case to my attention," Walter affirmed. "And according to this police report, you attest to the validity of the examiner's decision that Neil Darden died of natural causes. Who was the medical examiner at the time in question?" The mood in the room had changed, it sounded more like an interrogation was going on, with Walter on the interrogating side.

"I'm not exactly sure," Frank mumbled angrily. He took a resentful sip from his whiskey and set the glass down on the desk.

"What do you mean you're not sure?" Walter pressed.

"Well, F.C.P.D. wasn't the first on the scene. When I got there the place was crawling with government types. They were all sifting through Neil's personal belongings. And when I mean sifting, I mean they were pretty much just tearing the place apart," Frank explained. "I was furious. First because I had no idea who these people were and no one would give me any answers. And second because they were destroying a crime scene." He plucked a long thick cigar from a wood box and lit it, spewing smoke out of his nose and mouth in long whimsical columns. "Would you like one?" Frank asked.

"No thanks, I never could stand smoking cigars," Walter replied pulling a cigarette from his case and igniting it. "Continue," Walter said waving his arm from left to right implying he has the stage.

"Well, when I finally found someone who would talk to me and asked them for I.D., he said that they were government employees and that the F.C.P.D. had no more jurisdiction on this case, as far as investigating goes," Frank said. "I started to get really pissed off. I demanded to see some physical identification. And when he refused, I got even more mad."

"What did he do?" Walter asked.

"Ha," he laughed. "He got really close to my face and got extremely serious. He told me that Neil Darden had died naturally, and that was what I was to report to anyone that asked. Or else!" Frank said puffing on his cigar, unleashing another plume of smoke.

"Or else what?" Walter prodded. It was all starting to make sense to Walter now.

"Well…the man didn't say. He just looked down at Neil Darden's corpse and looked back up at me. I knew what he meant though. Interfere and die." He paused and looked around the room. "Never in the ten years that I have been Detective have I ever been that nervous. Whoever these people are, they're big. Real big."

"So do you think that they're trying to cover up these murders?" Walter asked. Frank's eyes shifted around and tiny glistening beads of sweat trickled down his face.

"No," He put bluntly. "With exception to the unprofessionalism, everything seemed in order. I had no reason to believe at the time that there was any foul play. "

"Then why did you threaten Edward Brussels the same way that these men threatened you?" Walter asked.

"Ha. You've been talking to Eddie too?" Frank asked rhetorically. "That man is a damn fool. I didn't threaten him. I simply relayed the message I got from the government officials, or whoever they were."

"My sources say you threated him with death, and slammed him up against the wall," Walter said.

"What? I did nothing of the sort. I was there for less than five minutes. I told him that the case was closed and that higher-ups have control now. Then I left." His voice became much louder. Franks sternness was a window that Walter could see right through. On the other side of that window, fear. An obvious kind of fear, masked with sheer, intense, uncontrollable anger. Not a good thing after a couple stiff, straight shots of whiskey and ice. "And just who the hell are you, huh? Coming into my office and accusing me of bad detective work," Frank said trying to change the direction of the conversation. Frank jammed his cigar into the ashtray on the desk. Embers were sent flying in all directions from the furious force. Walter sat silently. "You used to be a good cop Walter. We were the best team on the force. What happened to that?"

"You started drinking heavily. You

The Umbras

became a complete asshole. You pretty much gave up on yourself. I wasn't going to let that happen to me," Walter said defending himself.

"We're not all perfect Walter. Sometimes things happen that can't be changed. You need to understand that," Frank said bringing his voice from a raging torrent to a calm sprinkling.

Walter and Frank had a long history together at the F.C.P.D.. They had once been partners. In those days, either one would have taken a bullet for the other with no second thought about it at all. They would probably still be partners today if it hadn't been for Frank's actions on the last case they worked on together.

A murderer with a deadly obsession for young girls. He got his kicks by raping and torturing the girls to death, then leaving the bodies in school playgrounds for other children to find. A sick, sinister man, void of all feelings. For months Walter and Frank had nothing for leads. Then they got the tip they were looking for. A man named Charles Knebly was the murderer, they were sure about it. They had a name, an address, witnesses, and a murder weapon with matching fingerprints. All was quiet when they arrived at the scene. Frank banged on the door like only a cop knows how.

"F.C.P.D. Open up Knebly. We have a warrant," Frank yelled. Frank stepped out of the way and Walter kicked the door down, throwing shards of wood and metal into the air. Standing directly across from the Detectives stood Charles Knebly. He stared at the detectives, completely silent in the shadow of the room. He held in his arms a very young girl. Her hair was stained with blood, and fresh cuts ravaged her forehead. She was covered in some sort of bed sheet that had been crudely torn to fit her, much like a poncho. This too was stained with excessive amounts of blood. The young girl was trying to cry out for help, but Charles had his left hand pressed so tight over her mouth that only a muffled sound was allowed to escape. Walter was first to notice the six inch bowie knife Charles had up against the young girls neck. Charles was pressing the knife so hard up against the girl's neck that a small stream of fresh blood slowly dripped from her neck.

The Umbras

"Charles, please put the knife down and release the girl," Walter said calmly, training his .357 magnum sights directly onto the center of Charles's irregular shaped forehead.

"Get back, I'll do it. You know I will," Charles yelled, swinging the knife around at the detectives. His hair was a wild brown mess, covering only half of his head. The sweat poured profusely. His eyes were shaky, unsure, confused, and disturbingly blue. The jean overall's he wore were soiled with a random assortment of stains. All blending together to make a sort of grimy tie-dye effect.

"Drop your weapon or I'll shoot," Frank hollered, his gun already aimed at Charles. Tension was building as the three men and the little girl continued their stand-off.

"Put the guns down or she's dead," Charles yelled backing away from the detectives. His actions were frantic, much like that of a rabid, cornered cat. Charles Knebly knew his reign of terror was coming to an end. And he was more than willing to end it with death right then, and right there. "If you think for one second I care about her or myself, your wrong."

"Listen Charles, we can talk about this," Walter bargained.

"There is nothing to talk about," Charles replied.

"I will shoot you if you don't release the girl," Frank repeated.

"Frank, don't push him. Just wait for a minute, I think we can handle this without any violence," Walter whispered to Frank. The hammer of Frank's gun clicked as Frank cocked it. "Frank," Walter yelled. "Don't do anything stupid."

"You'd better listen to your partner," Charles added smiling ferociously and taking another step away from the detectives. Frank had had enough with this situation. With one swift movement, he squeezed the trigger of his gun and let out one, very powerful bullet into Charles's head.

"Frank, no," Walter screamed, frozen with shook. Charles swayed, still holding the girl. With the last bit of life left in him he brought the blade of the knife cleanly into the young girls throat, spewing blood everywhere. Charles hit the ground with a very loud thud. The young girl fell to the floor with Charles and tried to scream, but the laceration proved to be too deep, only a gurgling sound was emitted from her mouth. Walter ran over to the girl and tried to put pressure on the wound, but to no avail. She died in his arms with a sudden shudder. Her eyes turned into a cold steel blue. Lacking the normal luster a child's eyes hold.

"What have you done Frank?" Walter yelled. Frank stood silent, still holding his gun in the same position. He had made the wrong decision, and it cost a young girl her life.

From that point on, Frank became a raging alcoholic. He separated himself from Walter, and internalized all his problems. Walter could no longer watch Frank's self-destructive life. The partnership was over. Walter decided to start his own Private Detective business, leaving Frank to his own demise. The two detectives never really talked much about the last case they worked on together. They just went their separate ways.

The Umbras

"I understand that the past can't be changed Frank, more than anyone," Walter answered. A long moment of silence followed. A very awkward silence. The kind that only gets more awkward as time passes. Finally Walter asked, "So, what do you think about the injection wound on the victim?" The question caught Frank off guard a little.

"Now you're starting to sound like Allen Black," Frank replied, with a little hint of humor in his words.

"I'm sorry, who?" Walter said. His eyebrow almost reached the brim of his fedora.

"Allen Black.," he put bluntly. "He's this whack-job conspirator that's constantly harassing me with conspiracy theories. You know the type."

"Yeah…I know the type," Walter stated.

"He called me when he got word of the Darden death. The son of a bitch knows about everything we do here. Anyway, he said he had some information on the so called, 'killers', but I was sure of the legitimacy of the case, so I never called him back," Frank explained. He sifted

The Umbras

through one of the many stacks of papers on his desk. "Ah-ha, here it is," Frank said handing Walter a small, folded piece of paper with black ink visible from the heavy ink seepage. "That's Allen's home address. I'm sure you'd get a kick out of him. Or at least some useless information."

Thanks Frank. I do appreciate it," Walter said. He stood from his seat and extinguished his cigarette in the ashtray.

"Oh and Walter," Frank said as Walter opened the door to his office.

"Yeah?" Walter replied.

"Be careful out there." A concerned look flashed upon Franks face for just a moment as he said this. Walter stood in his door, not saying anything. He just stared into Frank's eyes. The eyes of a man he had left behind years ago. The eyes of an old friend. In the place, where it all started.

Derek E. Keeling | 50

The Umbras

Chapter 4
The Shadows

Derek E. Keeling
The Umbras

The late afternoon air was crisp. The fog lifted from the ground like the uncovering of a blanket. The deep, orange setting sun attempted to warm the earth, but was fruitless in its endeavor. Evening dew soaked through Walter's aged dark brown Top-Sider shoes as he walked through the winter grass outside of Allen Black's property. "Son of a…," he whispered shaking off the excess moisture from his shoes. He could feel the wetness penetrate his socks.

Allen's property was grand, to say the least. A secluded complex tucked away from the rest of the world. There wasn't another person around for at least five miles in all directions. A giant fence with razor-wire surrounded the entire fortress, with signs that read: No Trespassing, Keep Out, and Beware of Dogs. Walter didn't see any dogs anywhere within his viewing range. A very small house dotted the inside of the complex. It appeared to be built into the shape of the letter, L. Two tall radio towers stood behind the house and poked at the sky like the skeletons of a weathered obelisk. The house was made of red brick that showed signs of deterioration. And the roof of the house was completely flat, like that of an office building. An eerie English Ivy clung to the outside of the house, engulfing most of the sides with an elfin green color that seemed to accentuate the faded brick red exterior. A single window was cut out of the ivy incrusted wall. Pale venetian blinds shielded the view to the inside. A single gate, locked from the outside, by a chain and padlock, offered the only entrance to the property.

Being denied access to the house, Walter decided to walk the perimeter. Tall, dying weeds lined a path that encircled the fence. He followed the path intently, searching continuously inside the property for any signs of Allen Black. In the distance, he could see the shape of a man. He was kneeling down on one knee facing the fence. He appeared to be doing some sort of work on something, but it was unclear at that point. Walter silently crept up on the man, not to scare him, but to catch him off guard. He could see a head full of brown hair. It was flattened down and parted toward the left side of the head, and just barely inching it's way over the tops of his ears. The man was skinny and tall, this could be seen even as he crouched toward the fence. Walter came to within about seven feet of the man and said, "Excuse me." The man jumped up to his feet and turned to face Walter.

"Whoa! Where'd you come from?" the man shrieked. His eyes were wild with fear. And his posture was that of a man ready to fight for his life, or run for it.

"I'm sorry. I didn't mean to startle you.

I'm looking for Allen Black, are you him?" Walter asked. The man stepped back a few steps and eyed Walter up and down.

"Who are you?" he asked rhetorically. "C.I.A., F.B.I., what?"

"None of the above," Walter chuckled. "I'm Private Detective Walter Pierce. I was wondering if I could ask you some questions about a case you said you had information on."

"What case?" the man said curiously. He took another step back, still showing a lack of trust in Walter.

"Detective Frank Barlow said you called him in regards to the Darden case, is there any validity to this?" Walter asked. A fierce look came across the man's face as he asked this.

"Listen man, I don't know anything. I haven't seen anything either," he begged, slicing his hands through the air. "Just please, leave me alone. I won't say anything to anyone ever, I promise."

"No, it's not like that. I'm really just a detective. Here take this," Walter said handing the man his credentials. He studied the badge closely for a moment. A quick and fierce breeze came from the north, blowing the man's hair away from his face. The man took a shallow breath and looked around. His piercing eyes appeared to be a solid black and deeper than the deepest of all wells known to man. The dilation of the pupils was simply phenomenal, like the sun in full eclipse. He handed the badge back to Walter. He said nothing for a moment. His mouth moved as if he was silently talking to himself, but no sound came out. It was like he was trying to make a decision about the legitimacy of Walter's credentials. "He's obviously more of a paranoid person than I originally assumed," Walter thought.

"Follow me, it's not safe out here," he whispered. "We'll talk inside. And yes, I'm Allen Black."

The chain and padlock made a loud clanking sound as Allen unlocked and pulled it from the fence.

"What's that for?" Walter asked.

"It keeps the unwanted out," he stated simply.

"Ok," Walter said ending the conversation. They walked the path from the gate to the front door of Allen Black's house. Allen stuck a key into the door and unlocked the handle. Then he proceeded to unlock the three dead-bolts that adorned the door. The issue now, seemed to be the hardest one of them all. Allen Black just stood there. He didn't turn the handle and go inside, he just waited, with his back turned to Walter, silent. "Is there a problem?" Walter said curiously, stepping forward toward Allen.

"Well…," he whispered. Another silence followed. "Never mind, it's nothing. Please, come in." He finally gripped the handle to the door and turned it. The door swung open to reveal a mess of paper and wires. The entanglement of wires covered most of the furniture and floor. A rainbow of colors twisted and turned around his small house. "Sorry about the mess, I've been working," Allen said pushing a pile of papers off a chair and sitting in it.

"Working on what?" Walter asked as he closed the door.

"Nothing of importance," Allen replied. He pushed another pile of papers off a half rusted folding chair. "Sit," he offered, brushing his fingers through his hair. The room was lit like an old tavern. One lamp sat atop an old end table. A small lamp, with a bronze base shaped like a tree. Layers of dust covered the lampshade, making it hard to see the lush forest green color underneath. The light bulb had definitely seen better days. It shone a dim caramel color throughout the room. A few rays were allowed to penetrate the mess for the sheer purpose of general lighting. It made it hard for Walter to be able to tell where he was in the house: a living room, a bedroom, or a bathroom.

"So, what do you know about the Darden case?" Walter asked bluntly.

"Wow, right to the point," Allen said

leaning back on two legs of his chair. The chair released a high pitched squeal, like fingernails dragging slowly across a chalkboard. "So, I guess I'll get right to the point as well," he uttered sarcastically. "I have an idea as to how Neil Darden was killed, and who did it." He waited for Walter's approval with a child-like grin.

"Ok, go ahead," Walter said. He could tell he was going to get a lot of useless information, as warned by Frank.

"Alright. Have you ever heard of, The Umbras?" Allen asked. Judging by the tone of Allen's voice, Walter sensed Allen's enjoyment, and eagerness to explain.

"No, I haven't," Walter answered. Allen sighed with disappointment.

"The Umbras are an underground, shadow government agency. They work for the sole benefit of deleting people that interfere with their," he stated then paused. He continued, "with their objectives. I've heard everything, from taking out people that are in politics, people that invent something that's a little too ahead of its time, everything. There is simply no discrimination with them." The lamp started to flicker, dimming and brightening in odd rapid pulses. Allen lifted his foot and stomped the ground, sending a violent shake throughout the room. The light stopped flickering and returned to its normal dim self. "I hate it when it does that," Allen added.

"Neil's wife, Marcia, kind of told me about them. She said Neil was into that kind of stuff, and basically said he kind of feared for his life from them. Uh…What'd you call them?" Walter said.

"The Umbras," he put simply. "Umbras is Latin for shadows. So it's, The Shadows, essentially."

"I see. Do you mind if I smoke?" Walter asked, getting ready to light up a cigarette.

"Ooh…Actually, yes, I do mind. Those things kill you and everyone else around you. Don't you know that?" Allen cautioned.

"Yeah, I know. I just don't care," Walter said putting the cigarette back into his case, and then into his inside coat pocket.

"Thank you. Now, where was I?" he asked under his breath. "Oh yeah. So, these Umbras are apparently, well, apparently they are not human."

"What? What are you talking about?" Walter yelled, shocked at such a bogus accusation.

"Wait, now hear me out. I worded that wrong. They are humans. But, from the research that I have done, everything seems to say that they are…unlike humans," he uttered slowly.

"What do you mean, unlike humans?" Walter asked, completely confused at what Allen was saying.

"People say they have sharp or pointy features. They say that their noses look as if they are sharp. Now, not just like they have a knife for a nose. But a real human nose, chiseled to a point. Same goes for the ears and chin. Sharp and pointy seems to come up in every account," he explained.

"What people? Who are the ones reporting all of this information? I mean, if these killers are a group of shadow assassins, killing off everyone that gets in their way, then who is left to report the info?" Walter asked. "It's kind of like that dream where your falling off of a cliff, but you wake up before you hit the bottom. And it felt like you were really falling. Some people say if you hit the bottom before you wake up, you die. But, if that's true, then who has survived the fall in their sleep and lived to tell about it? Or, if it's true, where are all the dead bodies? The ones that were found splattered in their beds," Walter pondered.

"Damn man, I just tell it like I see it. There is probably a lot of lies in the stuff I research. But, that doesn't make all of it false," Allen justified.

"Your right, I'm sorry," Walter humbly acknowledged. "Please continue."

"So…Umbras, Umbras," Allen repeated, trying to remember his place in the story. "Oh, yeah, pointy noses. So, besides the sharp, pointy features The Umbras are, my research also tells me, extremely pale. Almost see through. And their skin fits really tight to their face. They all wear the same clothes: oversized black trench coat, black slacks, black shoes, and a black extra wide brim fedora."

"Do The Umbras also go by the name of the Men In Black?" Walter said jokingly. Allen stared at Walter with a look of disgust.

"Please don't patronize me," Allen replied defensively.

"Sorry, I was just joking. Come on, you got to admit they sound just like them," Walter said laughing a bit.

"Well, so does a ninja if you describe it right," Allen told Walter. "As I was saying. Their eyes are the only thing not described directly."

"What do you mean?" Walter asked, puzzled at this comment.

"May I?" Allen asked, pointing at Walter's hat.

"Uh…Sure," Walter answered. He gently took his fedora off and handed it to Allen. Allen nodded at him and cracked a slight smile, thanking him without words.

"All the reports said that no one has ever seen The Umbras eyes," Allen said. He placed the hat atop his head and pulled the brim down so that only his nose stuck out. "They all said that the hat covered the eyes. Completely covered the eyes, not even enough for them to see out. Which is odd, don't you think?"

"Yeah, it would be pretty hard to see your target when your hat is covering your eyes," Walter observed. "So, how do you think The Umbras killed him, and why?" Walter asked. Allen took the fedora off his head and handed it back to Walter.

"I don't know why they did it. I guess he must have been into some pretty deep stuff to get the attention of The Umbras. But, I don't know, that's for you to figure out. What I do have, is an idea as to how they did it," Allen said. Walter held the fedora in his hands, rubbing the brim between his thumb and index finger.

"Let's hear it," Walter said, nestling the hat onto his head.

"They use an untraceable poison, or, so we think. What I'm trying to say is, when a body is found that is suspected to have been taken out by The Umbras, it'll have a small injection hole at the top of the spine. But after all the tests come back, nothing is found. So, whatever they use to kill people with, doesn't show up in any tests. It's like whatever it is, kills the person and then dissipates, leaving no trace evidence," Allen explained.

"Interesting. The mortician ran some tests and said he found results that showed a toxin in Neil's body. Something unknown to science, as he put it," Walter said.

"It couldn't have been The Umbras then," Allen stated.

"Why?" Walter asked.

"Like I said, The Umbras toxin doesn't leave a trace, period," Allen said. His eyes flared toward Walter, insuring his statement was true. "It's that or the mortician you talked to has a new and more thorough way to screen people for toxins, which is probably not the case."

"I was talking to Frank Barlow about this. He said that when he showed up to the crime scene, there was already a crew of people there going through Neil's belongings. He also said he couldn't get any identification from them, but besides that they seemed legit. As far as you know, do The Umbras operate this way?" Walter asked.

"No, absolutely not," Allen said stunned at the question. "The Umbras, as far as I know, operate only in the shadow of night. And, as far as I know, they operate alone. Having only one person to get caught, makes deniability a lot easier for them. And besides the needle mark on the neck of their victims, they leave no evidence. None. Also, the people who share their stories or experiences about The Umbras, all end up crazy. I don't mean crazy literally, I mean they were literally locked up in mental homes and deemed crazy, or they disappear altogether," Allen explained. "The Umbras make sure that anyone that has any information about them, is considered a menace to society, so nobody believes it, or they snuff them out."

"So based on the fact that Eddie found a toxin when he ran his tests, which is abnormal. And the fact that there were unidentifiable people rifling through the crime scene, also abnormal. So based on this information, would you say that The Umbras did or didn't have a part in this crime?" Walter asked.

"I'd say based on all that, The Umbras had no part at all in the death of Neil Darden," Allen said with confidence.

"Do you know anything about the secret project Neil was working on?" Walter asked. Allen's head cocked to the right with great interest.

"No, never heard about it," he asserted.

"Well, Marcia told me that he was working on a secret project with one other person, at some unknown place," Walter explained.

"Unknown?" Allen said in a confused tone.

"Neil was so secretive, he wouldn't even tell his wife where he worked, or who he worked with." Walter continued, "She thinks he was probably murdered by his co-worker. She didn't say those words exactly. But, I could see that's what she was getting at."

"Why would his co-worker want to kill him?" Allen asked. Before Walter could get any words out of his mouth, Allen added, "And furthermore, why would they try to imitate The Umbras."

"I'm not sure," Walter said gazing at a pile of wires mixed with various articles of clothing. "They must think they have a good reason."

"Hey, listen, I don't mean to be rude or anything but, I kind of have a lot of work to do. So unless you have any more questions," Allen said, standing from his chair.

"Yeah, okay. I should probably get going anyway," Walter declared. "I wouldn't know it from in here, but I think it's getting dark outside." He stood from his chair and shook Allen's hand. "Thank you for your help. Please feel free to call me if you come across any information you think I should know about." He handed Allen a business card and headed for the door, almost tripping on a snag of extension cords wrapped in old, fraying duct tape.

"Let me get that for you," Allen offered. He held the door opened and stood beside it.

"Your gates not locked, is it?" Walter asked. He pointed at the closed metal gate.

"No, it's unlocked. Drive safe," Allen

said. Walter left the house and headed down the path. He could hear the sound of the front door slamming shut. A series of locking sounds followed, then silence. It had just begun to get dark outside. The cool evening breeze kissed Walter's face as he slowly opened the gate to Allen's compound. The sun was low on the western horizon, and only a sliver remained. It was slowly slipping away behind the distant hills. A few rays of sunlight beamed through a section of trees, scattering across the land like a disco ball.

    The only place Walter was able to find to properly park his car, was about a quarter of a mile away from Allen Black's property. The walk back was peaceful though. Walter enjoyed the brief moments in time when he was alone with just his thoughts. He was always contemplating things: life, the cases he worked on, women. He could see the silhouette of his car in the distance, about twenty yards away. He could also see the silhouette of another vehicle. "Who the hell is that?" Walter thought to himself. He focused his eyes as he walked closer. He could now see that it was definitely a van. A black van to be exact. With no windows on the backs or sides. About ten yards away, Walter began to run toward the van. His feet kicked up dust on the dirty trail leading to the gravel parking lot. He noticed the window on the driver's side door was slightly opened. Not enough to see in, but enough for the person inside to hear Walter as he screamed, "hey, stop right there." The van's tires squealed and kicked up tons of dust and smoke. Walter tried to see what the license plate number was, but with all the dust and commotion, he failed to see it. The smell of burning rubber filled the air instantly. "Stop," Walter yelled again. The van's tires had now gripped the gravel road and sped away at a very fast speed. The whole ordeal shot rocks and debris all over Walter's car. His windshield was cracked beyond repair, with a few decent sized holes where rocks penetrated. The car's body received numerous dents and paint chips. But this was the last thing on his mind as he quickly got into his car and started the engine. He put the car in drive and stepped on the gas. The car's back-end lost control and slid toward the left side of the tiny gravel lot. He tried again, but still the car slid. "What the…," Walter mumbled to himself. He stopped the car and turned the engine off. He knew what the problem was, he just didn't want to believe it. The car door swung open and Walter stepped out. "Son of a…," Walter yelled as he kicked the back left tire of his car, which was still spewing air out. A gaping stab wound adorned the tire. "Who the hell was that?" Walter wondered.

Derek E. Keeling
The Umbras

Chapter 5
Downtown Drive

Derek E. Keeling

The Umbras

The Umbras

"What a night," Walter whispered to himself as he checked his mail in the hallway that leads to his office. He pulled his keychain out from his right coat pocket. A various assortment of all types of keys. He searched for the small, brass key. It was always the easiest to find, as it was so small. He held it up to the mailbox marked: Detective Walter Pierce. The key scratched at the keyhole, missing Walter's every attempt to enter. Finally he entered the keyhole and unlocked the mailbox. The old, copper colored, metal mailbox creaked as Walter swung it opened. The inside was empty, as it usually was. He slammed it shut, sending a sound wave through-out the hallway.

The night before was rough for Walter. He decided not to bug Allen Black for assistance. Instead, he called a tow truck to come and get him. The truck took two hours to reach him. While he waited, the rain started. First it was a slow drizzle. Then after a few more minutes, it picked up to a downpour. Walter could do nothing but wait inside his car, which was leaking water through the newly broken windshield. He made it into town with no problems once the tow truck driver finally arrived. But, then the problem was getting his car fixed. The man at the auto body shop informed him that he would have to take a loaner car while they worked on his car for a day or two. The car was a pile…to say the least. A beat up two door hunk of metal. The interior was ripped to shreds. It seemed like every few inches there was a cigarette burn, or a stab wound. The car ran terribly. When it started the engine would smoke. It was only a little bit, but it was a dark black. Plus, the car had barely enough gas to get Walter to the gas station one mile away from the service station. Needless to say, Walter did not enjoy any of the experiences he had that night.

His office was stuffy. It was small, so it wasn't hard to make it that way. Walter opened the window and turned the fan on. It stuttered a few times before it kicked into full gear. He pulled a cigarette out of his case and placed it on his lips. An orange flame shot out of the lighter, burning the excess paper on the tip of his cigarette. He sat at his desk and breathed deeply in the smoke of the cancerous stick.

His mind raced with thoughts. He wondered about the van he had encountered the night before. "Who was that?" he thought, "and why were they there? Were they watching me, or were they watching Allen?" The thoughts ran around his mind like a rat in a maze. Something big was going on, and he was clueless as to what. None of the pieces seemed to fit. The more about the case he found out, the less he seemed to know. He picked up the police report and began studying it thoroughly. Still, nothing popped out at him, nothing made sense. Was this case doomed to be, unsolved? Was the original cause of death, the actual cause of death, or was there more to it? Walter pondered these thoughts as he went over the report.

A loud ring from the phone jolted Walter out of his concentration. The phone rang loudly again, struggling at the end of its ring with an almost whimper sound. Walter sat still, and did not answer. It was a kind of weird policy of his to make the person wait three rings before he picked up. He did it just to see if the caller was dedicated enough. Another ring was let out of the antique. Walter swooped it up like a bird on its morning prey.

"Detective Pierce," he stated. "How may I help you?" The voice on the other end didn't reply. Walter could hear the sound of someone breathing. It wasn't like the sound of creepy breathing, but more like the sound of urgent breathing.

"Walter, it's me, Thomas," the voice finally answered.

"Thomas?" Walter asked.

"Thomas Webster. You met me a few days ago at the morgue," he replied.

"Oh, yeah. Thomas Webster," Walter said, remembering the slightly chubby man that confronted him in the alley next to the morgue. "What can I do for you?"

"Something has happened that I think you should know about," Thomas said. Thomas's tone of voice put a sense of urgency into the air. Walter sensed it instantly.

The Umbras

"What?" Walter asked. He took a drag from his cigarette and blew it toward the fan. The airflow from the fan sucked the white smoke toward the window. The smoke swirled slowly and loosely at first. But as it got closer the fan, gathered tightly and swirled fast until it was eventually sucked out of the office and freed into the outside world. No words were uttered for a moment.

"Marcia Darden is dead," he put bluntly. His forwardness came as a shock to Walter. He quickly sat up in his chair.

"Wait, what? She's dead?" Walter wondered. "How? When…?"

"Look, just get over to the morgue and we'll talk about it," Thomas urged.

"Alright, I'm on my way," Walter said. He heard a click in his ear as Thomas hung up. He did not move, physically. But, his mind moved with rapid translucent thoughts. The kind that don't really make any sense, or don't stay long enough to really understand them. Kind of like the mind of someone who is afflicted with A.D.D..

The Umbras

He was confused, distraught, to say the least. "Why would someone kill Marcia?" he thought. "What the hell does she have to do with any of this?" He grabbed his coat and hat and headed for the car.

The loaner car wasn't going to give Walter a break just because he needed to be somewhere. Instead, it just puttered and popped as he tried starting it for the third time. A plume of black smoke billowed out from under the hood of the car, rich with the smell of burning oil. Walter pumped the gas pedal gently as he turned the key, the engine grinded loudly, followed by more popping. After a few more tries, Walter was able to get the car started. His hand firmly gripped the gear shift and put the car into reverse. As he backed out of the parking lot, the car vibrated violently, shuttering throughout its frame. Walter pumped the gas once more and brought the car back to life.

Downtown Francis City, relatively speaking, is a very small area. Consisting of three named streets, and thirteen numbered avenues. All three of the named streets were one block

The Umbras

west or east of each other, and the numbered avenues were one block north or south of each other. Both Walter's office and the Morgue resided on the same named street: Carter St.. Carter St. was situated west of the other two named blocks: Main St., and Portland St. Walter's office was on the corner of Third Ave. and Carter St.. The morgue was just an earshot away from Walter's place of business, located on Twelfth Ave. and Carter St.. So the distance between the two is very small. It would normally take Walter about fifteen minutes to get from his office to the morgue, and that is with all the traffic, stop lights, and the usual thick fog that hung around the city like cobwebs in an attic.

The fog parted slightly as Walter put the car into drive and headed south on Carter St. to the morgue. He reached up to the rear-view mirror to adjust it and noticed a car behind him start up and it's headlights turn on. He wasn't sure if this was just a coincidence, or if this happened to be something more. So he studied the vehicle behind him the best he could in the rear-view mirror. At this point all he could see

The Umbras

was the bright glow of headlights as they shone through the fog behind him. The stoplight on the corner of Third Ave. switched from green, to yellow, to red, forcing Walter to stop and observe the mystery follower. As the vehicle came closer, the features were easily made out. A tall black van, minimal windows, with just one person inside, the driver. The fog made it impossible for Walter to make out who was inside. But he knew this just had to be the van that was outside Allen Black's property.

As Walter realized this, he became very anxious. His eyes shot back and forth from the solid red stoplight, to his rear-view mirror. A wet, salty drop of sweat beaded down the side of his head. He wasn't sure why he was nervous, or scared. The feeling just hit him like a ton of bricks. His mind raced. "Who was this person? What did they want? Were they the ones that killed Marcia?" he thought. These questions trampled over each other in Walter's head, creating more fear, and more paranoia. The stoplight seemed to take forever. No cars were coming in either direction, yet the light was still red for Walter and the van. His hands gripped the steering wheel with nervousness until his knuckles were white. Finally the light switched, sending a vivid green cascading throughout the fog. Walter quickly stepped on the gas pedal, sending his tires into a sort of spin before they gripped the asphalt. The van followed Walter's move and also stepped hard onto the gas pedal. The van's tires screeched and spun, echoing throughout Third and Carter. Judging by the vans actions, Walter now knew what he was up against. He was being followed by The Umbras, and the thought thoroughly scared him. As far as Walter was concerned, he was on the verge on getting deleted, or silenced. He was not going to let this happen.

The loaner car sped down Carter St., in between Third and Fourth Ave, with the van following quickly behind. Walter's nervousness was running amuck, fogging his mind like the streets around him. Faintly, through the thick fog, a green light began to emerge. With one hard push of his foot, the car sped up to forty miles per hour, sending an unusual vibration throughout the car. "Come on baby, don't do this to me now," Walter uttered. The light had begun to change. The vibrant yellow pierced through the windshield of the car and left a glow upon everything. Walter blasted through the yellow light just as it begun to turn red. He had hoped that driver in the van would feel it was too dangerous to run the red light, and thus letting Walter get away unscathed. But unfortunately, the mysterious black van just kept on driving, completely avoiding any regard to the safety of himself or others. "Okay, it's time to pull out the big guns," he whispered, putting his seatbelt on. It was a normal thing for Walter to forget his seatbelt, but in this situation he thought, "I'm probably going to need this." The seatbelt made two clicks as it was forced into the receiver, the strap instantly tightened to Walter's chest and waist.

    The cars raced down Fourth and quickly made it through the green light that awaited them on Fifth Ave.. Walter tried to scan the next street for any oncoming traffic as he braced himself for the surprise he was going to pull on the van behind him. But, the fog was too thick. Nothing could be seen clearly, except the red light that faced Walter. He hoped that no one would be coming in the opposite direction. As he got closer to Sixth Ave. he noticed the headlights of traffic. A deluge of fear ran through him. His eyes peered into the rear view mirror to check the vans position. It followed close, swerving back and forth in a menacing manner, as if trying to taunt Walter into stopping and succumbing to his fate. Walter had no intension of stopping. The red light suddenly changed to green as Walter and the van approached. He spun the steering wheel violently and the sound of screeching tires filled the streets as Walter took the corner onto Sixth Ave.. The sudden violent left turn caught the chaser off guard. He had almost missed the turn. But, he veered sharply left. The driver adjusted his speed and took off not far behind Walter.

Sixth Ave. was a rundown street to say the least. Transients, prostitutes, gangs, and drugs all littered the streets. It was the street where most of the action happened when Walter was working with the Francis City Police

Department.

It was his intension to floor it, passing through Main St. and then taking a sharp right onto Portland St.. But, as he approached Main St., he could vaguely see the faint silhouette of a shopping cart being pushed by a homeless man, and a few more people crossing the intersection on the east side of the street. Thinking fast, Walter slammed on the brakes, sending the car skidding across the first crosswalk before the intersection, west of the street. Noticing this, the pedestrians scattered like bugs away from the scene. The only thing left in the intersection for this split second as Walter skidded and turned, was the homeless man's shopping cart that he had left behind. Walter gripped the steering wheel and took a quick left. The car felt as if it was going to flip as he turned the corner of Sixth and Main, but it didn't. As the vehicle skidded through the intersection, turning violently to the left, it smashed into the shopping cart that was left abandoned. Bits of trash, cans, and other debris shot across the back and side of Walter's car. He checked his rear view mirror again and saw that the van had anticipated the turn and made it with no trouble. "I've got to lose this guy," Walter thought as his car shifted itself into second gear. Walter, now heading north, truly put the pedal to the metal. The car, on the other hand, strained at such a request. A loud pop and a burst of sooty black smoke was expelled from the exhaust pipe. But still the little loaner car sped up faster, its weak aluminum frame rattling more and more as the speed increased. The van's speed was also increasing, gaining quickly on Walter's little loaner car. Both cars flew through Fifth and Main effortlessly.

The van's fog lights turned on, sending a blinding white incandescent beam into the car, enveloping all of Walter's view of the chaser behind him. For a moment his vision was completely blurred, stunned from the bright lights. "Oh yeah," Walter whispered. "How about this."

The asphalt shredded the loaner car's tires as Walter braked into the corner of Forth and Main. Smoke and rubber particles surrounded the intersection. The sound and

The Umbras

sudden chaos at Fourth and Main ceased for a brief moment, but Walter soon broke that silence and peace with another round of screeching and smoke as he turned onto Fourth Ave.. The van had to slam on the brakes, but over corrected and was sent spinning into a quick three-sixty degree turn. Walter peered into the mirror and saw that the chaser was stopped for just long enough to possibly make an escape. So, he extended his foot all the way to the floor and the car was sent flying down Fourth Ave.. Walter could see nothing through the thick fog as he hit speeds in excess of fifty miles per hour. "Time to lose this fellow," Walter thought. The car started shaking again as the speedometer reached sixty miles per hour.

The corner came fast. Almost too fast. A garbage truck out on its normal route was trying to take a left turn from the east side of Fourth and Portland. Walter had just enough time to react. As he laid hard into the steering wheel for the right turn from the west side of Fourth and Main, the garbage truck slammed on his brakes. Walter swerved just enough to miss the truck and jolted right passed the front of it. Walter heard the sound of screeching tires behind him. "Ha," Walter bellowed, happy with the sudden turn of events. The van was completely stopped, stuck with the garbage truck in front of him. The garbage truck driver was in a state of shock from the situation that had just occurred. Needless to say, he wasn't moving.

Walter could barely see the garbage truck and the mystery van, which were still stopped at the corner of Fourth and Portland. The image started to disappear into the fog. Walter's nerves were still shot, but he felt better being further from the situation. The Umbras scared him, he wasn't sure why. They just did. The car sped down Portland St., passing easily through Fifth, Sixth, Seventh, and Eighth Ave.. Until Walter felt he had completely lost the van.

As Walter approached Twelfth Ave., he couldn't help but feel a little stupid for letting himself get as scared and nervous as he did. He also couldn't help but feel dumb about the whole car chase in general. "I'm a cop, well, a detective I guess. I shouldn't be running from someone, breaking every law in the book. I should be chasing them," he observed. The thought of this eased the pressure from his foot to the gas pedal. The car slowed down quickly, as if yearning for torpidity. The stop light on Twelfth Ave. glowed brightly green into the fog. Walter took the right turn with ease and calmness. It was over, seemingly. He could see the morgue ahead, passed Main St. and on the corner of Twelfth and Carter. The building was like a trophy for Walter, shining in the distance. It was a kind of solace to him. That was until he thought about poor, sweet, beautiful Marcia Darden. The late wife of the late Neil Darden.

    He pulled into the parking lot. The loaner car popped one last time as he turned the engine off. He sat in the car thinking for a moment. His mind wasn't thinking of anything specific, just running through everything that had just happened. Kind of like a slideshow of the day, little pictures in his head passing back and forth through his mind's eye. All amounting to nothing, just mental rhetoric. He got out of his car and entered the morgue.

The Umbras

The door to the mortuary had just slammed shut as the black van pulled onto the road next to the morgue. The headlights went out and the engine turned off.

Derek E. Keeling

The Umbras

Chapter 6
Another Morgue Mystery

Derek E. Keeling | 90
The Umbras

The putrid smell of the morgue had greeted Walter's nostrils the moment he entered the building. It was a fragrance that can never be forgotten once whiffed. An absolutely nasty mixture of rancid meats, eggs, and curdling milk. All of which filled the air and mixed with whatever cheap, flowery air freshener was on hand at the time. "Glad to see the place hasn't changed much since I've been gone," Walter said to himself as he wiped his feet on the dusty gray doormat. With exception to the horrid smell, he was beginning to feel safe, calm, and comfortable. The chase had stirred his fears into a frenzy. His manliness, he felt, was shattered into a pile of childish pieces. He ran like a coward fearing for his life. But a sense of security came over him as the adrenaline settled within him. The creepiness of the morgue, had turned into a safe haven for him.

A long, dimly lit, straight corridor laid in front of Walter, fading into the dark distance of the morgue. A glimmer of gold to his left caught his eye as he finished wiping his feet and started down the hallway. A very simple plaque, made from a cheap metal, and containing large black letters that read: Presentation Room. To his right was the office of Edward Brussels. One window allowed a view into the room. Walter peered through the thrashed venetian blinds and found only darkness. The hallway extended passed two exam rooms, and soon came to an intersection where another hallway led far to the left and the right. He stood at the intersection of these hallways and looked around. The place seemed to be deserted. No movement, no nothing. Just silence, and stillness. Down the hallway to his right, he noticed three doors. Two of which, looked like normal doors. But the third, looked to be an emergency exit of sorts. He could see a red sticker atop the door, but couldn't make out the writing.

 He could hear the sound of a door opening behind him. It jolted him out of his staring stupor. He turned sharply and could see the familiar pudgy shape of Thomas Webster, the mortician's assistant. He was drying his hands off from a recent wash. The damp paper towels shuffled back and forth in his small, sausage-like fingers. He looked up and met eyes with Walter from down the hall.

 "Walter, you made it," he said still

wiping his hands, this time with increased speed. "What took you so long?" he said as Walter decreased the distance between them.

"It's a long story," Walter said shaking his head.

"Well, never mind that, please come with me," Thomas said with urgency. He jammed the paper towels into his back pocket and led Walter through Exam Room Three's door.

The room was cold, bitterly cold. Stabbing through Walter's thick trench coat with ease. A shiver was sent throughout his body, giving him goose bumps.

"Why is it so cold in here?" Walter asked, tucking his hands into the deep pockets on the front of his trench coat.

"Keeps the bodies fresh," Thomas answered. Bodies were everywhere, littering the room like the scene from a horror movie. All the bodies were placed on stainless steel gurneys, which adorned the entirety of the room. A stark white sheet covered them. Stains appeared randomly on the sheets, some deep crimson, some smoky yellow. "She's over here," Thomas said. He walked toward the back right of the room to a table shoved into the corner. A sheet with numerous stains, varying in color, blanketed the body. Walter could see a few strands of blond hair exposed from the sheet, laying gently on the cold steel table. The sight sickened him. He turned from the body and covered his mouth, his face beginning to turn a light shade of green.

"How did this happen?" Walter asked, repulsed at the image before him.

"Well…Hey are you okay?" Thomas said, just noticing Walter's unusual state of illness.

"Yeah, I'm fine." He shook the feeling away from himself and faced the body and Thomas. "So, what going on?"

"She came in about three hours ago," he said, placing his right hand on his chin. "She's got a needle mark on the back of her neck, like Neil." He paused and scratched his chin and neck. The excess fat and skin made a wave-like movement that seemed to cascade down his face like a receding ocean wave. "But, unlike Neil, Marcia has a bit more bruising, and a few more needle marks."

"What are you saying?" Walter asked.

"Well, I'm saying that there was a struggle. Here, take a look," Thomas said. He grasped the stained white blanket with his hand and pulled it down to Marcia's chest. "You see here," Thomas said, pointing to a bruise on the lower part of her chin. The bruise was nasty, with a deep purple center, fading out to a pasty yellow-green.

"My God," Walter exclaimed. A sickness fell upon him the instant Thomas revealed the body. Walter was normally good with seeing and dealing with dead bodies, with exception to the smell. But seeing Marcia laying stiff and cold on a steel table did something weird to his insides.

"You see these needle marks, how they don't go in straight. Based on that, and the bruising, I'd say that there was a struggle before she succumbed to her fate," Thomas reiterated. Marcia's body was riddled with small needle holes. Some of which, appeared to have entered sideways and left a long streak of red where the puncture was made.

"So, why did you call, me?" Walter asked.

"I wasn't supposed to call you," Thomas answered. His eyes paced across the body of Marcia Darden, studying her with visual rhetoric. "I just thought it was necessary for you to know."

"What do you mean by you weren't supposed to call me?" Walter wondered.

"When the body came in, I first called Eddie. When I told him about the marks and bruises on her, he told me not to tell anyone," Thomas said. "But, I thought you ought to know, considering your involvement with this case."

"Why didn't Eddie want anyone to know about it?" Walter sought.

"Past experiences, I guess. He was probably just scared," Thomas answered, unsure.

"What about the police, what did they do?" Walter said curiously.

"Ha. The police did the same thing they did last time, closed the case.

"What?" Walter said stunned. "How is that possible?"

"They said it was a suicide. According to the F.C.P.D., she injected herself and died in that warehouse," Thomas answered.

"How does that make any sense? Did they find the needle? Why was she at the warehouse in the first place? All of these are good enough questions to keep a case open," Walter said furiously.

"Someone is making it so all of this just

goes away, just disappear," Thomas said. "Whatever's going on, no one is supposed to know, or supposed to find out. And if they do, they end up like the Darden's." His chubby fingers stretched out and pointed toward the late Marcia Darden.

"Ok then, I've got some work to do. Do you know what warehouse she was found at?" Walter asked pulling out a small pad of paper and a pen.

"Yeah, the old abandoned warehouse on the corner of Third and Portland," Thomas answered.

"Is that the building with the sign that says, Young's?" Walter asked.

"Yep, that's the one," Thomas said.

"Well, I can't thank you enough for all your help, I do appreciate it," Walter said humbly. Walter's hand extended outward toward Thomas's.

"No problem," Thomas said, shaking Walter's hand tightly. "Be safe out there."

The door shut behind Walter, slamming and echoing throughout the halls. Walter's sickening feeling only increased as he walked toward the exit through the halls of the morgue.

As he walked by Eddie's office, he glanced into the window to check to see if he had arrived. The room was still blanketed in darkness. It was as dead and as cold as the bodies in Exam Room Three. The horrid mass of flesh that lay still, lifeless, and pale, brought frightening feelings to Walter.

"Am I next?" he wondered. The door handle turned and released its catch on the frame, exposing him to the consistently gray, foggy, and dark interior that downtown Francis City was known best for. A whipping breeze stung at Walter's cheeks. He was tired of the cold. He was tired of the unknown. He was tired. But the work had to continue. If he stopped or rested now, more victims could turn up, including himself. With this in his mind, he shoved the key to the loaner car into the ignition, starting a series of rattles and pops that jolted and frightened him. He was most certainly on edge. His hands started to shake, not violently, but enough for him to be concerned for himself.

"Get ahold of yourself," he quietly whispered. The engine popped one last time and finally started. Walter let pressure off the key and put the car into drive. One push of the gas pedal sent the car flying out of the parking lot.

The black van soon followed Walter's lead and started up the vehicle. This time the van's lights stayed off. He pulled onto Twelfth far behind Walter. Walter saw none of this, oblivious with fear.

Walter took a deep breath, trying to calm himself. He tried to shut out the fears with rational thoughts. "This is bullshit," he thought. "Someone is toying with me, trying to hide something." He gritted his teeth tightly, exposing a long tough muscle along his jawline. "The Umbras are a myth," he tried asserting to himself. But still he had his doubts. He wondered who would go to such extents to silence the people that got in their way. No answers came to him as he took a left on the corner of Twelfth and Portland St.. The long expanse that is Portland St., faded away in the distance behind a shroud of thick, white, Francis City fog.

The long rectangular building took up the land from Third and Portland St., to Second and Portland St.. It extended one city block wide, with a parking lot paralleling it and Portland St..

The light turned green and Walter pulled into the vacant lot. There was not a soul to be seen. He saw an entrance to the building and parked near it. The car shut off without any problems. He sat in the car, unsure. Unsure about what he was going to find in this place, if anything. He figured if the F.C.P.D. closed the case without thoroughly investigating the scene of the crime, then maybe, he might find something worthwhile.

Chapter 7
The Photograph

Derek E. Keeling
The Umbras

The Umbras

Long stringy strands of yellow and black police tape hung in a criss-cross fashion on the main entrance doors. Police Line Do Not Cross, written in bold black Helvetica stared at Walter, warning him of his trespasses. A feeble attempt at exclusion. Thick fog encompassed the space between Walter and the door, almost becoming a barrier in itself. But Walter, without any hesitation to the warning written in black, violently ripped the shiny plastic tape from the door and threw it onto the ground.

"What the hell am I doing here?" he thought. "Nothing makes any sense anymore? Why did they pick this place to kill her?" He was confused and distraught. A state of confusion mixed with a slight dosage of paranoia crept upon him, shrouding out his rational thoughts for a brief moment. "Why was she here? Was there a reason?" he wondered.

He jiggled the door handle, hoping that it would be unlocked, but to no avail. He took a quick glance around the area to see if anyone was around that would spot him breaking into the building. Still, there was not a soul to be seen. And even if there was a person lurking in the darkness, the fog was so thick that no one would be able to see, or be seen.

He readied his shoulder for the impact,

and in one swift motion, lunged into the weak plywood door, tearing it cleanly from its frame. The sound reverberated throughout the warehouse. And the slap the door made as it savagely slammed to the warehouse's cold cement floor, pulsed through the building like a hundred people slamming their foot down simultaneously in a vast cathedral. Regardless, he was in. The interior of the massive metal building was mostly dark, with a few spots that were a shade or two lighter than the rest of the warehouse.

"What the hell is that?" Walter whispered. He stood staring at a stack of something large and oddly shaped, but he couldn't make it out. The dark was thick, mimicking the outside fog, and Walter's unadjusted eyes didn't help the situation. He squinted toward the tall shape about twenty feet in front of him, trying to force his eyes into defeat. As he began to walk closer, the shapes became clearer. A perfect stack of what appeared to be boxes. "Packing crates," he said, not amused with the find. He smacked the wooden crate with his hand. His confusion and paranoia had unexpectedly turned into anger. He wasn't sure why, it just had. A deep breath came from the Detective as he tried to calm himself and continue with what he came for. Whether or not there was anything at all was a burning question in his mind. But it could only be answered, it could only be satisfied, by continuing his search of the vast warehouse.

As he walked past the wooden crates, he looked up. He noticed that the entire warehouse was open, with only one upper area. In comparison to the entirety of the warehouse, the solitary room was tiny. "Probably an office or something," he thought to himself. Two windows could be seen on the side of the room. Walter looked around to try and find the way up. But as he did this, something shiny caught his eye from the far opposite corner of the building. He decided to try and find the entrance to the room after he investigated the mystery. He walked diagonally across the warehouse, scanning the area as he went. Nothingness, pure nothingness. Whatever they did in this warehouse was an enigma to Walter. The emptiness appeared unbounded.

Within thirty seconds, Walter was standing in front of a mass of shiny, yet rusty barrels. Numerous fifty-five gallon drum barrels were shoved, with no apparent order or reasoning, into the corner. He looked fervently around the drums, searching for anything that could make some sense of this case, or at least point him in the direction of something that would make sense. But he found nothing, he just stood against the barrels with his head down, frustrated with the way things were going. But giving up was never his way, nor was accepting defeat in the pursuit of justice.

Walter could see a set of metal stairs leading up to the room that hung in the warehouse. He could also see something else, directly across from him. It had the shape of a car, but with other accentual features. He quickly paced toward the mystery. About ten feet away from the mystery, and to the left of Walter, he noticed a huge metal bay door. The kind of door used for bringing in huge trucks or huge payloads of material. The door was slightly ajar, and fog could be seen trying to sneak in from under it.

Continuing through the warehouse, Walter was now within visual range of the mystery vehicle. A cluster of stout, bright yellow forklifts neatly parked in the corner of the warehouse. Feeling like the office held more potential for evidence or clues, Walter turned for and headed toward the stairs that led up ten feet to the room.

A rigid rebar-like staircase, cold and sharp, stung at Walter's exposed hands as he tightly gripped the handrail. The room had a sign above the door that read, Office Employees Only. Walter turned the handle to the door, and threw it open.

"Glad I don't have to break another one down," he thought rubbing his shoulder which ached with pain. "That's definitely going to bruise," he whispered.

The office was a shell of a room. Nothing but a few folding metal chairs and cheap drywall, stained a dull yellow from cigarette smoke. Atop the center of the room was a circle that was nicely stained into the wall, the old resting place of an old clock. "It seems even time is gone from this place," he thought. He blew a breath of resentment out, followed shortly thereafter by a sigh of disapproval. He was starting to feel regret for showing up in the first place.

"Wow, what a crime scene," he thought with utter bewilderment. Just as he was about to give up on the seemingly frivolous search in the office, something small and brown caught his eye. He bent down, and with one eyebrow arched picked the object up. It was a very small brown cigarette filter. All of the tobacco had been smoked and all that remained was a stub of a filter. Walter examined it closely with studied eyes. He began to fidget with the butt, trying intently to consider its value. He stood for a moment and then placed it into his pocket. It was his only piece of evidence so far, and he wasn't going to let it go, regardless of how menial it was.

Suddenly, he heard a quick and quiet metallic sound come from outside the small room. Slowly, he crept across the office and down the stairs. His eyes were now fully adjusted to the darkness. He peered across the warehouse, with the utmost attentiveness, scanning left to right for any sign of movement, or anything that seemed unusual. But he didn't see anything, just an empty void of a warehouse. He took a couple steps forward, still scanning for movement. A dark spot on the cement caught his eye. It stood out in contrast to the sheer gray concrete below his feet. His eyebrows perked up and he started walking over to the spot. As he began to kneel, it became clear what it was that he was looking at. His eyes focused onto the stain and he noticed tiny drip marks surrounding it. Blood, the blood of the beautiful and late, Marcia Darden. This he was sure about.

To see her poor, pale face dressed with death was a shocking image for Walter. The weird thing was, he had seen many dead bodies before, most in worse shape than she was. To Walter, her beauty, and her death, should have never been. It was like seeing the ripest, juiciest and most luscious fruit you'd ever seen, smashed to pieces right in front of you.

He examined the blood stain closely, looking for any signs of a trail. But there were no drips leading off in any direction. He stood, and after taking his fedora off, briskly scratched his head. A shower of dandruff sprinkled onto Walter's shoulders and the cement floor. His lack of personal hygiene was a testament to his commitment to the case, weirdly enough.

His eyes veered toward the forklifts, searching for a blood trail. He turned slowly to his left looking meticulously on the floor. When he made it back around so that he was facing the stairs to the office, he saw it. A few dark drip-like spots dotting the stairs and handrail. As he drew his eyes down from the stairs, he saw a few scattered drips heading from the steps toward him and the stain of blood. It was obvious what had happened now. He could tell the struggle began either in the office, or on the stairs themselves. Marcia's blood starting dripping out onto the stairs as she came down them, and finally ending up where he stood, where she died. It became clear to him.

"I probably missed something in the office," he thought. His eyes were randomly led to something under the stairs. It looked like a small square piece of paper. Perplexed at this, he headed for it, desperate for a physical piece of conclusive evidence.

Then from behind him, the quick fading in of a very familiar sound, footsteps. They came so quick and so quietly that Walter barely had time to react. He swung his arm around as he tried to face the attacker, slamming it into the attacker's arm and hand. The clink of an object hitting the ground echoed in the warehouse.

Before Walter could fully turn to face his assailant, an arm had wrapped around his neck and begun to squeeze tightly. He choked as the pressure increased. The two fumbled a few steps toward the forklifts. Walter could feel it coming. The inevitable loss of consciousness one has when oxygen enriched blood fails to reach the brain. He felt he only had one chance, and this was it. He mustered up all his energy, and with one clumsy movement, rushed himself and the attacker quickly toward a parked forklift. The result was devastating. The attacker slammed into the forklift with all the might and force of Walter's push. His grip was loosened a lot, but he still had a hold. Walter breathed in deep, trying to regain full control of his consciousness. But, just as the one breath he took was satisfying his need for oxygen, the assailant regained his grip on his neck. Walter slammed the attacker against the forklift once more, this time knocking the arm away from his neck completely. Walter coughed violently, his body was screaming for air.

    In a flash of a moment, he heard the attacker running away from him, obviously feeling like his efforts were ineffective, and further pursuits would be frivolous. Walter tried to follow, but tripped as he began his pursuit, still coughing and dizzy. He watched the man slip under the small opening in the bay doors. There was no point in pursuit, he could barely see straight. His lungs were tight and felt as if they had just caved in. The cold temperature in the warehouse reveled Walter's attempts at taking deep breaths. A wispy pillar of cold white air left the aspirated body of Walter Pierce and spread throughout the general vicinity, eventually dispersing into the very air in which he was seeking. After a brief moment of trying to regain his equilibrium, he brought himself up from the floor.

His mind raced with fears and uncertainties. "Was that The Umbras…?" he wondered, still slightly distraught from the incident. Building up all the energy he had, he staggered toward the partially open, warehouse bay doors. He was not content with the early escaping of his attacker. He needed, as a Detective, to follow the man, and if not apprehend him, obtain some form of evidence to continue his pursuit of the assailant. But, just as he arrived at the bay doors, the loud sound of tires squealing and skidding off filled the air. Walter suddenly dropped down to his hands and knees, which stirred up a flurry of dust and sediment. His head peered out into the open street, disturbing the resident fog around him, which seemed to revel in the idea of movement in a sea of still, condensed fog. Walter, on the other hand, despised the thick droplets of water vapor that appeared to suspend themselves on the invisible cushion of air they surrounded. He could just barely see the dark black shape of the van as it took a left on the corner of Second and Portland St.. Because of the fog's ability to limit visibility, he was unable to clearly make out the license plate number on the back of the van.

"I'm in this too deep," he thought. He was beginning to realize the gravity of his situation. Whomever it was that wanted him dead, was probably the same person, or group of persons, that had killed both Neil and Marcia Darden. With this in mind, Walter was unequivocally certain that they would stop at nothing until he was out of the picture. He all at once felt powerless and scared. An extreme sense of helplessness came over him with sudden rapidity.

He sat with a slight chill in his bones and a fever of fear running through his veins. It boiled within him like water at sea-level. The dust cloud he had stirred up had begun to settle back into its place, dancing to and fro like miniature snowflakes on the way down to the floor. His knees and elbows were covered in a thin layer of dust.

As he stood from his extended stupor, he remembered what he was previously doing before the confrontation with the attacker. He humbly locomoted across the warehouse from the bay doors back to where he was investigating the blood drippings. The ordeal was over, and regardless of his nervousness, or lack of willingness to continue, he tried to pull the strength from deep down inside him. This, of course, came in the form of a small, shiny, rectangular cigarette case. He pulled out a long cylindrical filtered tobacco stick. It's tan filter was covered in tiny, beige colored, misshapen spots, resembling that of an odd tiger. The translucent white paper, reveled a dark brown tobacco in a crosshatch like pattern. His bony hands fumbled with the lighter, trying desperately to catch a flame. Pieces of red-hot flint scattered through the air like a volcanic explosion as he numerously scratched at the flint-roller. After many failed attempts, Walter cupped his hands around the lighter and cigarette, and after taking a deep breath, as if to breathe away his anxiety, caught flame to the lighter. The flame was brought near to the cigarette, and before it reached it fully, the residual heat lit up the exposed excess paper in a fiery blaze of orange and yellow. He drew in deep, satisfying and calming his shaken nerves and burned up adrenaline reserves.

"The paper," he thought with extreme enthusiasm. He took one more drag of his cigarette and tossed it onto the ground, sending hot ember shrapnel throughout the vicinity. He had forgotten about the paper momentarily because of the distraction he suffered. As he began to pick the pace of his walking up, another thought rushed into his mind. He suddenly remembered what happened right before the attacker starting choking him. The sound echoed through his mind like music in an system of cathedral like caves. He remembered the sound of the clinking that he heard as he threw his arm into the assailant's hand. He rushed over to the area where the incident took place. His eyes frantically searched the hard floor for any sign of an object. As he made his way over to where the forklifts were parked, he noticed something under them. He bent down to pick it up, and before his hand touched it, he quickly drew back. The item he saw only affirmed his theory on who tried to kill him. Walter stared down at the horrifying sight before him, a short syringe with its plunger fully drawn. The deadly liquid concoction remained inside the barrel of the syringe, shining up at Walter with a light auburn gleam. A short silvery needle protruded from the end of the barrel. It was a menacing sight for Walter to see. He then realized the seriousness of his situation, and he was slightly disturbed by it. He knew that if it wasn't for his quick reaction, he would have been stuck with the needle and probably dead. Another victim to the mysterious Umbras.

      He fumbled through his trench coat

pockets, looking for anything to hold the deadly needle. His hand grazed a cold metal object, and as he pulled it out, he realized what it was.

"Keep one for myself," Walter whispered as he dumped the contents of his cigarette case onto the ground. He shoved the single cigarette he saved behind his ear, and then he pulled his fedora down onto it to keep it in its place.

He bent down to pick the syringe up with his cigarette case. As he scooped the evidence into the case, a small amount of the liquid in the barrel squirted out from the needle. It splashed itself onto the inside on Walter's cigarette case and the surrounding cement ground. He tried closing the lid to the case, but the plunger was out just a little bit too far. Walter knew he needed at least some of the liquid in order to do proper testing, without it, there would probably be little or no evidence on the syringe. He slowly pushed the plunger in, spilling a few squirts onto the internal area in the case. The plunger cleared the case without having to push all of the liquid out of its barrel. He snapped the case shut with extreme urgency. He placed it back into his pocket and stood up from his kneeling position.

Feeling satisfied with obtaining one piece of evidence, Walter headed over to the stairs where the piece of paper was. He could see it laying directly under the stairs as he walked toward it. The rattle of the syringe in the cigarette case was music to Walter's ears. "Finally, some real evidence," he thought. The stairs were completely open on the underside, which would allow Walter to easily reach the piece of paper. As he squatted down beside the staircase, he could slightly make out what the paper was. A photograph laid in front of Walter. The white backside was facing up, hiding whatever photo was on the other side. He extended his left arm into the space between the stairs and the wall, reaching with all his might to grab the photo. His middle finger just barely touched the picture, sliding it close enough for him to get a firm grip on it. He turned the photo over as he withdrew it from the underside if the staircase.

    He stood from his crouched position and focused on the photo. The picture was faded with age. There were two men standing in the foreground of the picture shaking hands, appearing to be celebrating something. Both men were wearing clean-suits. A very loosely fitting, full-body garment used to keep germs, bacteria and other contaminants that are on a human body out of a laboratory. In the background was a very large building painted in a drab gray-like color. A huge red acronym sat atop the building.

    "C.A.N.D.L.?" Walter wondered staring intensely at the aged photograph. He had never heard of such a place. The picture itself confused him and made him curious as to the point and purpose of it. He wondered how the photo got to the location in the first place. After a moment of staring intently at the photo, he glanced down toward the bottom of the picture.

The bottom had a white strip of tape where someone wrote the words, Project Begins. Following the two words were a series of exclamation points. Walter felt utterly confused. He had assumed that finding this picture would bring some of the pieces of the puzzle together. But instead, brought on a deluge of questions. Questions that had to be answered. The only problem was, he was unsure as to how he should go about answering those questions. He knew that a group of shadow government, stealth assassins were hunting him, and anyone that tried helping him. So asking anyone for anything could become a death trap for both parties.

The door to the warehouse slammed shut and Walter walked toward his beat up loaner car. The car looked like Walter felt. As he got into the vehicle, he became worried that he might endanger anyone that he seeks help from. After a big sigh of disappointment, Walter's head hit the steering wheel with defeat. He was worn out, tired, and scared. But even more than that, he was confused.

"I need to find out where this C.A.N.D.L. place is, and pay it a visit," he thought lifting his head up from the steering wheel and starting the car. It started fast and strong. He pulled onto Third Ave. and started to head back to his office to recoup.

He felt that he knew less than he did when he came to the warehouse. Plus, he was now sure that he was being pursued by an extremely dangerous group of assassins.

Chapter 8

An Interesting Day

Derek E. Keeling
The Umbras

The Umbras

The next morning was cold. A violent shiver snaked down Walter's back as he opened the door to his office. He slammed the door shut with little or no regard for anyone or anything around. He was tired. He hadn't gotten much sleep the previous night. Most of the night he spent wide awake, paranoid that The Umbras were waiting for him outside his house. He wasn't able to get much thinking done with the fear of death firmly placed in his mind.

His eyes hung low, and rested sloppily on the dark bags that resided on the undersides of them. He was a mess. He was wearing the same clothes that he had been wearing the night before, and they were now covered in thick stains of dust and dirt. A few rips were scattered throughout his attire, revealing his sun deprived, white skin.

As he sat down in his torn up office chair, he picked the phone up. His long, rigid fingers slowly began to dial a series of numbers as he placed the phone up to his ear. He waited patiently as the phone rang. A sudden click was heard halfway through the third ring.

"Hello," he said, drawing the word out like a kind-hearted southerner. "This is Thomas Webster. What can I do for ya?" His attitude was cheery, the perfect kind of voice you would want, or expect, to hear when you call a place of business.

"Thomas, it's me, Walter," he said with a stern tone.

"Hey Walter, how are you?" Thomas asked cheerfully.

"I'm fine, but I really don't have the time or energy for pleasantries. I need some help and I need it as soon as possible," Walter said with even more sternness.

"Okay, okay. What do you need?" Thomas asked, sensing Walter plea for professionalism.

"I need you to analyze a piece of evidence for me, and I need it done in a few hours," he answered.

"Whoa, that's a tall order my friend. It's going to take some more time than that. What are we talking about here anyway?" he curiously asked.

"I can't really talk about it too much over the phone. I'd really rather try and keep the utmost discretion when it comes to this. I'll let you know more when I see you," Walter said. His eyes peered across his office and through the amber colored window that hung so dreadfully in the door. "I just don't want anyone besides you and me to know about this, for the safety of both of us."

"Alright then. Just come by my office and I'll take a look at it," Thomas stated.

"Okay, I'm on my way," Walter said. He hung the phone up and sat still for a moment. The echo of the phone slamming rang throughout Walter's office, penetrating his inner ear. His mind raced with thoughts. He knew that if he went outside, he might be jeopardizing his life, or the lives of others. But, he also knew that if he did nothing, the death of Neil and Marcia Darden would go unsolved, closed, and eventually, erased and forgotten. He gritted his teeth together, bringing every ounce of courage in his body to fruition.

"I need to stop acting like such a coward," he thought to himself. "It's time to step up to the plate, and bring justice to this case." His mind flipped one hundred and eighty degrees. In just a moment, he snapped out of his fear enduced stupor. The feeling of courage and bravery crept back into his soul, filling him until his feelings of paranoia disappeared into the very depths of his mind in which they came from. He felt as if he had been pretty selfish. His worries and cares seemed to be all about himself, and this wasn't his normal way. To Walter, being in danger was just another part of the job. But, for the past few days, he had forgotten about this. Now, with a fresh mind and attitude, Walter was ready to put his full energy and attention into this case.

The drive to the morgue was fast. Before

Walter left his office, he was sure that someone would end up following him to the morgue. The last thing he wanted was another chase. But, to his surprise, no one followed. He drove straight down Carter St. with a hint of reckless abandon. The majority of the street lights were green, allowing Walter to cruise briskly through them, and continue without much slowing down or stopping.

He turned into the morgue's parking lot from Twelfth Ave. The sun had just breeched itself over the perfectly rectangular building, casting brilliant yellow-orange light on the parking lot and Walter's car. A fervent ray of hot sun beamed itself through Walter's windshield and grazed his face with an intense heat, comparable only to that of a mid-summers day. With all the cold that had embraced Francis City in the past few days, he genuinely welcomed the heat with open arms.

The car rattled gently as he turned the key to the off position. He gathered the evidence that he was going to present to Thomas and exited the car. He stretched his body before he started walking toward the front doors to the morgue. A loud yawn was expelled from his rigidly shaped mouth, and a set of slightly stained teeth reveled themselves to the late morning sun.

The door slammed loudly behind Walter as he entered the main corridor of the morgue.

The hallway was an empty void, lacking both life and light. Walter looked around as he stood trying to adjust his eyes to the sudden darkness.

"Hello, is anyone here?" he yelled taking a step forward. "Thomas? Eddie?"

A door opened from down the hall, spilling the internal light of the room into the corridor. A chubby head popped out from inside the room.

"Walter, over here," Thomas yelled back. He began waving Walter toward the room. Walter followed suit and met up with Thomas at the doorway to the room.

"How are you today?" Walter asked with genuine kindness.

"I'm fine, just working on a cadaver," Thomas answered leisurely, trying his best at humor. A deep and exhausting sounding sigh came from Thomas. "So, what do you got for me?"

"Well, I was wondering if you could take a look at this syringe for me?" Walter said pulling out his silver cigarette box. He handed it to Thomas. Thomas's plump fingers grasped the box and opened it.

"What do you want to know about it?" Thomas asked curiously.

"Well, for starters, I'd like you to check to see if there are any finger prints on it. Then do a full toxicology test. I want to know what that stuff is, and possibly who made it," Walter answered with bold seriousness.

"And you want in a couple hours," Thomas said sarcastically.

"Yeah, as quick as you can," Walter replied. "Plus, I don't want anyone to know about this until I do, got it?" Walter said sternly.

"Okay, I can do that," Thomas assured. "I'll give you a call as soon as I get some results."

"Alright then, I'm going to get out of here. I need go get something to eat. I'm famished," Walter muttered.

"I got a couple of sandwiches in here if you want to join me," Thomas offered. "I wasn't planning on eating this early, but if you want?"

"Uh, no thanks," Walter said, laughing half-way through the sentence. "No offence, but, I really don't want to eat anything that's been in this place." A sort of sour look took over Walter's face as he said this.

"Have it your way," Thomas said reluctantly. "I'll call you soon."

"Okay, have a good one," Walter said as he turned from Thomas and proceeded down the hallway.

***

A chewed up chunk of chicken flew from Walter's teeth as he poked and prodded with a skinny wooden toothpick that he got after his lunch. He had taken his time at lunch in hopes that there would be some sort of news from Thomas when he returned to his office. And, as the door to his office slowly creaked open, he could see the signature flashing red light on his answering machine. He hoped it was the message he had been waiting for. He quickly closed the door to his office, took off his coat and sat in his chair. He slouched down in the chair and let out a sigh of relief, still full from his lengthy lunch. After fumbling through his pockets for a cigarette, which he realized he had none, he pressed the button on his answering machine to begin listening to the message.

A loud beep was released from the machine before the message started.

"Hey Walter, this is Thomas. I wasn't able to get a toxicology test run yet. But, I did find fingerprints. I ran them and." There was a brief pause in the message. "And, you're not going to believe this. The fingerprints were a match for…" At this point there was a loud grunt, followed by excessive noise and obvious struggling. Walter sat up in his chair attentively. The sounds of crashing, smashing and grunting lasted for just a moment, before a silence consumed the air around Walter. He listened fervently, waiting for any erroneous sounds. His head tilted toward the answering machine hoping to pick up more sounds that couldn't have been heard otherwise. At this moment, another loud beep was produced from the machine, ending the message. His skin seemed to jump from his bones as the sudden loud sound was emitted into the air. The noise surely frightened him.

He picked the phone up and dialed the number to the morgue. A busy signal was all he received from the call. After slamming the phone down onto its receiver, he sat for a moment, trying to think of not only what just happened, but also, what he was going to do about it.

He quickly stood from his chair and grabbed his trench coat. He knew that he needed to get back to the morgue and see what became of the situation that he had heard on his answering machine.

The loaner car started up with no problems. As he pulled out of the driveway onto Carter St., his tires squealed. A short black line of rubber trailed the car, eventually fading out into nothingness as the tires firmly gripped the asphalt. Walter put full pressure on the gas pedal, speeding the metal hunk to its maximum ability. It shot down the road, passing through numerous green and yellow lights. Conveniently, Walter encountered not a single red light on his way to the morgue. The streetlights glistened vaguely, trying hard to match the intensity of the bright sun, but to no avail. He sped past many cars, with the passengers glancing at him with concerned faces.

In just a few minutes Walter made it to the morgue. The car found its way into a snug parking space. A bit of smoke and steam came out from under the hood of the car. Walter had pushed the little loaner car to its limit, and it was showing signs of stress and wear.

"Great," Walter said, getting out of the car. He ignored the smoke and steam for the moment, deciding it would be better to just do what he came he to do. He knew he would have his chance to worry about the car when he was done.

He cautiously approached the front door to the morgue, unsure of what he might stumble upon. He unclicked his holster and placed his hand on his gun. His hand grasped the cold steel door handle and turned, freeing the door from its frame. As the door creaked open slowly, rays of light from the outside penetrated the interior of the morgue. A long dark corridor stretched itself out before Walter's eyes. It seemed to be just as desolate as his last time in the building. As he entered, his shoes made a sharp clicking sound that echoed throughout the hallway. The place was so quiet, he could hear his own breath spewing from out of his mouth. The tension, or lack there-of, sent an unsettling feeling through his mind. He crept with the fluidity and speed of a hunting lion, slowly moving in on its prey, with the utmost attention to movement and detail. This time, he knew, he was going to be the predator, not the prey. There would be no surprises. His eyes pierced the surrounding area with bold looks of anticipation. He wasn't sure what he would find, if anything.

As he approached Eddie's office, he noticed the venetian blinds were in a sort of unusual tangled mess. Behind the bent and broken blinds, Walter could see that the room was dark, enigmatic, and void of life, just as much as it was void of light. Walter quickly opened the door to Eddie's office and entered. His right hand searched for the light switch, finding it with haste and turning it to the up position. An overhead light flickered on, and sent rays of pale florescent white strobe-lighting across the room. Flashes of destruction and disorder littered the room in a furious display of chaos. Finally the light became still, as did Walter. His eyes could barely take in at in at first.

Sheets of papers, and a random scattering of the usual assortment of office utensils covered the entirety of the office furniture like snow. As Walter scanned with his eyes from left to right, his ears finally caught up to his mind, and he heard the familiar sound of a dial tone. He looked around, honing in on it like a falcon with its prey. A couple of feet in front of him he noticed, wrapped and tangled in a knocked over chair, the phone and its base. The place was disastrous, an obvious struggle had occurred, Walter was absolutely sure of this. He knew what he needed to do. Carefully, he stepped over a mass of debris and fetched the phone and its base. He hung the phone up for a quick moment and then lifted it to his ear. His long, skinny fingers pushed several of the phone numbered buttons, and a dial began.

"Hello," a deep and raspy voice said, followed by the loud sound of a veteran smokers cough.

"Frank, its Walter," he returned, halfway through Frank's cough.

"Yeah, what do you want?" Frank said in an overall displeasing tone of voice.

"Something has happened here at the morgue. I need you to put out an APB on Thomas Webster. He's gone missing," Walter replied.

"Well what makes you think he's gone missing?" Frank asked.

"Listen Frank, I don't have time for this," Walter said. "I just need you to do it."

"Well, I need something to go on. I can't have my guys just running around this great city like a bunch of chickens with their heads cuts off, now can I?" Frank said, increasing his tone to thoroughly angered.

"Alright, alright, calm down," Walter

said. "Thomas was running some tests for me on some evidence I've gathered."

"What kind of evidence?" Frank inquisitively asked.

"A syringe," Walter replied. Walter heard a sigh of approval and acceptance from Frank in the background. "I told him to call me when he got any results. I wasn't there when he did, so he left a message on my answering machine. When I finally listened to it there was a big struggle."

"Did he say anything about the results?" Frank asked.

"He began to, he was just about to tell me who the fingerprints on the needle were when the struggle began," Walter answered. "So, I drove down here to see what happened. I'm calling you from Edward Brussels office, where the struggle took place."

"How can you tell that?" Frank prodded.

"By the enormous amount of crap laying around," Walter said. "So are you going to help or what?"

"Yeah, I'll put an APB out on him. We'll find him," Frank said sincerely.

"Thanks Frank, I mean it. I owe you," Walter gratefully replied.

"Damn right. You owe me a round of beers, and a round of shots," Frank said with a groggy voice.

"Okay then, it's a date. I'll talk to you later," Walter said.

"Alright, you be safe out there," Frank said. A click was the last sound Walter heard before the room became silent and alone once again. The destruction, even though it hadn't left, felt to Walter as if it had returned.

After a pointless walkthrough of the entirety of the building, he left the morgue. He knew it was a dead-end, a place where there would be little evidence to be gathered. He pulled out from his brown trench coat the square shaped photograph with the mysterious C.A.N.D.L. building and two men shaking hands on it. He stared at the photograph as he sat in the loaner car, its engine struggling to run.

Derek E. Keeling
The Umbras

Chapter 9

C.A.N.D.L.

Derek E. Keeling
The Umbras

Derek E. Keeling
The Umbras

Walter slammed the door shut to the little loaner car and reached into his left pocket for a cigarette. He felt the square and sharp shape of the photograph and nothing else. But still, his hand shuffled around for a moment before finally withdrawing in defeat. He quickly felt the outside of his right pocket. He felt nothing, so he gave up.

"Convenient," he scoffed, sarcastically coming to terms with his lack of tobacco products. He felt it would be a good idea to smoke a cigarette and scan the place out before he embarked inside. But, because of the absence of such items, he decided to just go right on in.

The place was grand. The epitome of massive. A huge, oddly shaped white facility with long, black smoke towers bulging out of the roof. Any spot seemingly available had these stacks. The bold black color stood out against the unusually brilliant blue sky. Plumes of thick gray smoke bellowed from inside the belly of the long stacks, adding to the overall enormity of the place, both visually, and physically. Across the top of the building, in enormous black steel letters, C.A.N.D.L. could be seen. Under the mass of bulky letters read, Chemical And Natural

Development Laboratory.

This perked Walter's curiosity. He knew that whoever was killing, whether it be The Umbras, or someone else, was using advanced chemical technology. He knew he was getting closer to the truth, closer to justice. But, he wasn't sure what exactly he would find here.

C.A.N.D.L. was still an unknown to him. He had previously never heard of the place. He never would have found the place if he hadn't stopped at a phone booth on the way back from the morgue and looked it up. It was located dead center in an industrial area on the outskirts of Francis City. It was surrounded by similar looking buildings. All of which seemed to spew chemicals of different types into the air simultaneously. Walter drew them in deeply, substituting his lack of cigarettes for harsh breaths of chemical filled air. It did nothing for him, except bring an exasperated sigh out from within him.

He opened the door on the side of the building that he parked his car. As he entered the room, he immediately noticed the strikingly beautiful woman. Her eyes penetrated him instantly, forcing him to revel a scarcely seen smile. Her vibrant shimmery red hair was twirled into a loose bun that hung gracefully atop her head. A row of glowingly white teeth shone brightly across the room toward Walter. Her smile took his breath away. She wore an elegant black top that was nicely covered in glittery crystals. Walter could see the overhead light dancing in and out of the crystals as she moved gently in her chair. The top had a single strand of fine silken string connecting the front to the back. Her shoulders stuck out of the sides of the top. A beautiful freckled and pale blend of soft well-formed skin graced every inch of her visible body. Her lower half faded away under the neatly organized desk she sat behind. Walter stepped close to the desk. He was unable to speak on account of the bold beauty before him.

"How can I help you?" she cheerfully said. At first, Walter heard the words, but did not say anything. He just stood in front of her desk, silent, and creepily fidgeting with his hands. "Are you all right?" she asked, followed by a cute laugh. He realized how drone and inappropriate he was being, and snapped out of it. His head shook swiftly as if actually shaking off his stupor.

"Yeah, I'm sorry. It's been a long day," he replied blushingly.

"It's okay, I know how it is. So, what can I do for you?" she asked with a perky smile. Walter reached into his left pocket and retrieved the photograph from inside.

"I was wondering if you could tell me a little about this photo?" he said, presenting the picture to her. She reached out slow, and with angelic grace. Her eyes shuffled back and forth for a moment.

Then, she began to show another exquisite smile. As her full and pouty lips pulled away from her teeth like a curtain on a stage, Walter knew he was about to get some useful information.

"What and why do you want to know about it?" she asked.

"I'm a private detective investigating a murder case, possibly involving these men. I was wondering if you could tell me who these two men are?" Walter answered, pointing to the figures in the photograph. "And what this mean?" He stretched his hand out and pointed at the words, Project Begins. "Any help would be deeply appreciated." Her eyes became wide, and a surprised look changed the original shape of her face from cheerful and smiley, to distraught and concerned as quick as lightning.

"Oh, wow," she said. "That's pretty intense. I didn't expect you to say that."

"I apologize. I don't mean to put you on the spot like this," Walter said.

"No, it's no problem. I just didn't expect it, that's all," she proclaimed. She paused and took a deep breath, trying to calm her nerves from the initial shock of the situation. "The man here," she said, pointing to the man on the right of the picture. "Is Neil Darden, he was our Chief Engineer here. He was a great man, and a good friend of mine." Walter could see a wet look developing in her eyes. The kind of look that can be felt by anyone who sees it, anyone that has lost a true friend or family member. He felt for her, he understood the deep and painful effects of losing a loved one.

"I'm sorry for your loss. I know how hard it can be," he sympathized. A tear ran down her cheek and dripped from her chin. She wiped her face in embarrassment.

"Thank you," she said gratefully. She took another deep breath and wiped the remaining wetness from her face. "The other man," she continued. "Is Ed…" She was interrupted by a door swinging open and crashing into the wall.

The door was located to the left of Walter

and the woman's desk. A horde of men filed out of the door, shutting it behind them. All were dressed in stereotypical security clothes. A short-sleeved black shirt tucked nicely into a pair of perfectly ironed black pants. Each individual man had an assortment of gidgets and gadgets that adorned the gaudy leather belts they wore. Both Walter and the woman had an extremely surprised and worried looks on their faces.

"Please come with me," one of the men said sternly. "Your trespassing on private property." The man reached out and grabbed Walter by his arm. He squeezed tight and tried to pull Water toward the exit. But Walter jerked his arm free. "If you don't leave the building, we will call the police."

"We can do this the easy way of the hard way," another man said, stepping in close to Walter.

"I'm leaving, I'm leaving," Walter yelled. "Calm yourselves men," he said. He turned around and headed for the door. The men stayed in the room and watched him as he left the building. The door slammed shut behind him. He felt angry, like he had just been ripped off. He turned right and started walking toward his loaner car. "Ed?" he thought. "She didn't mean…? No, couldn't be." His mind raced with questions. As he was walking he noticed an outdoor ashtray receptacle to his right. He felt that he needed a cigarette bad enough to consider scrounging in the ashtray.

The ashtray was filled will butts of all sorts. As he shuffled through them, he kept close eye out for one that was big enough and had the least amount of damage. He spotted a nice long cigarette at the bottom of the ashtray. It had only had a few drags taken from it. It looked vaguely familiar to him. The dark brown filter with diamond patterns stood out in his mind like a sore spot. But he couldn't remember why. As he rolled the cigarette, checking for damage, the word, Fin, appeared. All at once Walter realized what he was holding.

"Oh my god," he whispered to himself. He reached into his left pocket and searched rapidly. Then, finding nothing in the left, switched to his right pocket. His fingers dug deep in the trench coats big pockets. He felt a small cylindrical item at the bottom of the pocket. He fetched it out and examined it in his hand. "Son of a…" he said. "It is Eddie." He held in his hand the small cigarette butt he found in the warehouse. As he compared it next to the cigarette he retrieved from the ashtray, he knew for sure it was a match. From what Eddie told him, he had these cigarettes specially imported, and they were rare and hard to find.

He wondered for a moment, standing vagrantly next to the ashtray in a state of bewilderment. All the pieces of the puzzle seemed to fall into place for him. All at once he could imagine how the evidence fit the crime and the suspect. He knew that he needed to take some of the cigarette butts with to get them tested to make sure that they were in fact, Eddie's. But, he knew they would be, it just made sense to him now. The only problem was, he wasn't sure of one, single solitary thing. One key piece of the puzzle that perplexed him greatly. He suddenly felt as if the puzzle was still not complete.

"Why?" he wondered. "Why do all of this?" He turned and headed for his car. He knew he needed to get to a phone so that he could call Frank Barlow and have him put out an APB on Eddie. Thoughts raced through his mind like a cat chasing a mouse through tight quarters.

As he drove aimlessly around Francis City, searching for the first phone booth he saw, he couldn't help but feel a little childish. He felt as if his assumptions and fears about The Umbras were misled. He also felt as if he fell victim to Allen Black's conspiracy theories. He knew that he wasn't normally the kind of person that could be so easily persuaded with rhetorically paranoid jargon. But he did, and he didn't like the idea of seeing himself becoming so paranoid over something as mythical and imaginative as The Umbras. A certain clarity also came over him. He felt good knowing that he was about to finally have his suspect within reach.

He turned the car into a dingy looking diner off the corner of Seventh and Portland St.. The place was the kind of diner you came to when you need something cheap, hot, and kindly served. But not the kind of place you go for good, quality food. Thankfully for Walter, he only needed to use the phone booth that was next to the entrance to the diner. It had an accordion-style door that allowed the user a sense of privacy when making a call. As he walked up to the booth, he glanced up at the sign on top of the small restaurant. Written in giant, red neon letters, the words, Vern's Diner. Some of the letters pulsed off and on, blinking endlessly in a feverish display of incandescence.

Walter opened the accordion-style doors

and a loud metal scratching sound was released into his ears. He clenched his body from the noise. It seemed to pierce deep into his mind through his ears. As he stepped in the booth and closed the door behind him, the sound returned. His body once again clenched at the sound. He picked up the phone and began to dial Frank Barlow's office. His fingers tapped the keys to the phone in a rhythmic pattern. With exception to the annoying sound he just heard, he was feeling kind of giddy about the whole situation. He knew that this was the call that would get the ball rolling. This would be the call that would bring justice to all the innocent people who had suffered or perished as a results of Edward Brussels actions. Walter understood that the families of the victims needed justice. The capture and indictment of Edward Brussels would do just that. The phone rang a few times before Walter heard a click sound.

"Hello," Frank said in his usual raspy voice. Walter could smell the stale cigar smoke and good quality whiskey on Frank's breath just by hearing his voice through the telephone. It certainly wasn't unusual for Frank to be halfway through a full bottle by noon.

"Frank it's me, Walter," he said in a sort of

calm voice. "Have you heard anything on Thomas?"

"No, nothing yet. His car is still parked at the morgue," Frank replied.

"Well, I think I know who the killer is," Walter said.

"Who?" Frank asked, perplexed by the sudden news. Walter heard the familiar sound of ice in a whiskey glass clinking around.

"Edward Brussels," he answered. A satisfying breath came from Frank's end of the phone.

"Based on what?" Frank asked.

"I followed a lead to a place called the chemical and natural development laboratory, or C.A.N.D.L. for short," he replied. "I asked the secretary that was there about two men in a photo that I found in the warehouse where Marcia was found dead. I was following another lead. She told me one of the men is Neil Darden. Right when she was about to tell me about the other man, the building security forced me to leave. But, she did get out part of the name. She said Ed right before they busted open a door and asked me to leave."

"Well, that's not really enough," Frank said with a hint of disappointment in his voice.

"There's more. On my way out, I was going to grab a cigarette butt from the buildings ashtray. I noticed that the cigarettes in the ashtray were the same ones that Eddie smoke," Walter said.

"A million people smoke cigarettes Walter," Frank said with the kind of tone a father gives his teenage son.

"But these cigarettes are specially imported by Eddie. Plus, I have a cigarette butt that needs to be analyzed that I found at the crime scene where Marcia was found dead," Walter added.

"Interesting. Do you have a motive?" Frank asked.

"That's the only thing I do not have. But, what I do have should be enough to have him brought in for questioning, right. I mean, if he did work with Neil Darden and didn't say anything about it to us, I want to know why." Walter pleaded.

"Yeah. So do I," Frank said.

"So you'll put out an APB on him for me?" Walter asked.

"Yeah, I can do that. But now you owe me big time," Frank said proudly.

"I know, I know. Don't worry about it, you'll get your beers and your shots soon enough," Walter said sarcastically.

"Alright then Walter. Unless there is anything else, I'm going to get back to work," Frank said.

"No, that's plenty. Thank you very much Frank. Call me when you hear anything," Walter said.

"Will do. Bye," Frank said.

"Bye," Walter said. He heard a click as Frank hung the phone up. He let out a deep breath of relief. He felt he had done all that he could do at this point. Now he just had to wait until Frank Barlow and his misfit crew of so called Police officers found and apprehended Edward Brussels. Soon, he hoped, he would be sitting in an interrogation room finding out the truth behind Eddie's maniacal ways.

Derek E. Keeling
The Umbras

Chapter 10

One On One

Derek E. Keeling
The Umbras

The next day was an agonizingly long test of Walter's patience. He spent most of the typical cold and foggy Francis City day lounging around his office. He aimlessly scanned and analyzed notes from the case, desperately searching for anything he might have overlooked. He threw down a small stack of papers onto his crowded desktop. He knew that he couldn't stop searching, even if there was nothing to find. He needed anything. Any motive or lead that would help bring Eddie to justice would be beneficial. He was not about to let Eddie walk back onto the streets of Francis City unscathed by the talons of justice.

As the day turned rapidly into night, he began to feel somewhat diminished. The more he thought about the situation he was in, the less he felt he knew about it.

"If Eddies the killer, who was the one behind closing the case so quickly?" Walter thought. He remembered that a group of high ranking, so-called, government officials, were at the crime scene. A thick haze of confusion swept over his mind. "Who would go to such extents?" he wondered. Then, he remembered The Umbras.

"Was it The Umbras, or was it C.A.N.D.L.?" he thought chillingly. "Maybe C.A.N.D.L. is The Umbras. Maybe The Umbras are C.A.N.D.L.?" he pondered in a soft whisper. The words slipped out of his mouth like he had just had an epiphany. His eyes sat still in their sockets, dead still. He felt a cold chill run down his back, blasting the calmness from him. He thought about Eddie, and how he was probably never going to get caught. "If he is part of some elitist government agency, they'll probably protect him," he said hesitantly. "Maybe even delete the entire situation. Including me." His mind flooded with thoughts. He had started biting his lip, but didn't even realize it. The veil of fear was beginning to take ahold of him again. It drew him in fast, and with furious precision, like an arrow to a bulls-eye. As soon as the fear had built up to an almost unsurpassable amount, the phone rang. Its loud cry snapped Walter out of his daze. The fear also seemed to disappear. Reality had quickly kicked in. He suddenly felt better, like a weight had been lifted off of his shoulders. He remembered that the fear one gets when becoming involved in a case is natural, something that comes with being an officer of the law. He released the pressure off of his lip. A white imprint with a red border remained on his bottom lip. The sound of the phone pierced the air like the shrill call of a bird of prey. Walter snatched it up from its base mid-ring. "Hello," he said.

"Walter, its Frank," the voice replied. The tone of Frank's voice sounded rough, as usual, but, at the same time, had a hint of excitement to it. "I've got some good news and some bad news. What do you want to hear first?" Frank asked

"Alright, give me the good news first," Walter said hesitantly.

"We've got Eddie in custody," Frank reveled. "I have some men in the interrogation room talking with him, or, trying to talk with him for that matter," he continued. "He hasn't said a word."

"Is that the bad news?' Walter asked hopefully.

"No, unfortunately it's not," Frank answered. He became silent. The only thing Walter could hear was the jagged sound of Frank's breathing on the other end of the phone. "We found Thomas in the trunk of Eddie's car," he said breaking his elongated pause. "Eddie was trying to flee town. He had Thomas's body wrapped up in sheets and tied in rope. The trunk also had a briefcase containing numerous syringes and vials. I'm assuming he killed him with an injection."

"Damn it," Walter yelled, slamming his fist unyieldingly onto his desk. The desk lamp rocked back and forth like an oversized, oddly shaped pendulum. "He didn't deserve that."

"They never do," Frank put simply. The statement shocked Walter just as much as it made him respect his former partner a little more.

"Yeah, I know," Walter said. "Where did you find him?"

"He was heading west on highway 26. He was probably going to ditch the body in the woods," Frank replied. "Listen, why don't you come down here and talk to him yourself. He isn't talking to us, maybe he'll talk to you."

"Yeah, that sounds good. I can be there in ten minutes," Walter said.

"Okay, see you then," Frank said hanging up the phone. Walter hung up the phone and sat motionless in his chair, stunned from the news. He was happy that Eddie was caught and in custody, but on the other hand, Thomas had paid the ultimate sacrifice for helping him. That made him a little uneasy. The longer he sat and thought about it, the more it made him furious. He needed to know why. He needed to talk to Eddie.

He left his office as fast as he could, almost tripping on the way out the door. The little loaner car, which at first was as troublesome as a car could come, was now an enjoyable piece of machinery to Walter. It started fast and strong, humming a hymn as Walter stepped on the gas pedal to leave the parking lot. The drive to the police station was quick, and heavily fueled by Walter's furious hunger to know the truth.

The car screeched into a parking spot in the oversized lot at the police department. A plume of black smoke followed behind and filled the air with a dense burnt rubber stench. Walter quickly exited the car and entered the building. His mind was racing. He could visually see everything in his mind. All the clues fit together in a beautiful sequence. All but one, why. It was driving him nuts. He walked past the front desk without being noticed, and headed straight toward Frank's office. His hand had just grasped the door handle to the office when he heard someone yelling his name from behind him.

"Walter, over here," Frank yelled again, this time louder. Walter turned around and saw Frank Barlow waving him toward the interrogation room. He was surrounded by Francis City's finest, all of which had very concerned looks stretched across their faces. Walter walked briskly up to Frank and his entourage.

"Where is he?" he asked Frank. The group of men surrounding Frank looked Walter up and down, sizing him up. It was a typical thing to do as a police officer. Walter knew this and took no notice to it.

"He's in here. He hasn't said anything yet," Frank affirmed.

"Okay, I'm going to go in and talk with him," Walter stated. "But first, I want you to take these and give them to your boys to analyze." Walter pulled the cigarette butts he had obtained from his left trench coat pocket. After giving them to Frank, he reached deeply into his right pocket and retrieved the small cigarette butt he found in the warehouse. "Run those against this. I'm sure you'll find some solid proof." Walter dropped the minuscule butt into Frank's hand. He turned from Walter and yelled loudly at the men behind him.

"You heard the man. Take this and get it done, now," Frank said sternly, handing off the butts to a bug eyed, confused looking officer. He turned and ran toward a hallway and quickly disappeared. "Okay Walter, I've got the tape running. My men will be in there with you to make sure everything stays peaceful."

"No Frank, I need to be in there alone with him. It's the only way he'll talk, I guarantee it," Walter bargained. Frank stood staring off into space, softly grinding at his jaw and in his mind.

"Alright Pierce. If anything goes wrong, I'm sending my men in to take care of it," Frank said. Walter only replied with a confidant nod. He held his hand out, beckoning Walter toward the door. Walter opened the steel door and stepped into the room. The loud sound of metal reverberated in the room as one of the officers closed the impenetrable flat sheet behind Walter.

"Hello Eddie," Walter said in a dronish tone. He pulled the chair out from under the square table that was in the middle of the room. He sat down and lit up a cigarette, blowing smoke directly at Eddie in an insulting, yet deserving manner. A large, highly reflective two-way mirror was the only thing that adorned the stark white walls of the interrogation room. The white walls were heavily accented by a bright white light that hung in the center of the room. Even with his brown wide-brim fedora, Walter still had to squint a little bit.

Eddie sat still and motionless, staring down at the table. He was impressively still. All except his left eye. It twitched with an evil fury. He looked as if he had snapped mentally. A large gathering of sweat rolled down his head and face. The sweat was like a deluge of concentrated fear and corruption. He said nothing. Barely even a breath of air seemed to fill him. Walter blew out another drag of his cigarette and flicked it into the ashtray on the table that was next to the microphone.

"Are you going to be silent all night?" Walter asked. "I got plenty of time. But, you have even more the way I look at it." Eddie wasn't even fazed. He remained completely solid, both in movement and in emotion. All but his left eye, it still twitched violently. Walter decided to try and change his tactics. "You know," Walter said. "You almost had me there in the warehouse the other day. And you almost had me convinced I was being hunted by The Umbras," he said with a humoristic tone. He let out a few chuckles and then took a long drag from his cigarette. "But you're nothing like them. You are way too sloppy," he said blowing out the smoke. "And weak," he added. At this point Eddie's left eye stopped twitching. An angry look came across his face. His eyes squinted at the table with a bold furiousness. It was like he was trying to burrow a hole into the table with his eyes and mind. He very slowly turned his head in Walter's direction. Both of their eyes met. A minute long stare-off then took place with both of them completely still. Walter could feel Eddie's eyes burning viciously into his. But he sent the same destructive stare back at Eddie in huge droves. Eddie's face started to morph into a nicer, more pleasant looking form. Walter felt confused, but continued to stare. Eddie cracked a slight grin and then he licked his lips disturbingly.

"Got an extra cigarette?" Eddie asked manically, breaking the long silence. Walter perked up and inhaled deep off his death stick.

He blew the smoke into Eddie's face. It hit his face like a baseball hitting a wall. Eddie sat with the same evil grin on his face, unfazed by Walter's insult.

"That's all you're going to get until you give me some information, understand?" Walter said calmly. Eddie didn't say or do anything in response to Walter. He just sat with the same ugly grin, staring deep into Walter's eyes behind a cloud of smoke. "Understand this Eddie. We already have enough information to put you away for a long time. So, you can either help me, or you can begin your time right now," Walter said in a threating manner. A cold face befell Eddie. A look of utter helplessness and acceptance, like the look a deer gives before it gets hit by a car. His eyes fell back down to the table and a glazed look came over them He knew he was done.

"I was only doing what I was told," Eddie confessed hesitantly. His eyes appeared as if they were climbing an invisible ladder back up to Walter's, stepping up a few inches at a time. After a moment, they finally met with his. "It was only supposed to be Neil. The others were…were mistakes." His eyes fell back down to the table and then closed.

"What do you mean?" Walter prodded. He glanced toward the mirror and opened his eyes wide. He did not expect it to be so easy.

"If everyone would have just stayed out of it, none of this would have happened," Eddie said.

"Stayed out of what?" Walter asked.

"You still don't know, do you?" Eddie replied.

"Know what?" Walter asked confused.

"Neil and I were working on a top secret project at C.A.N.D.L.. We were making a bio-toxin that could kill with extreme speed," Eddie answered. Walter sat up in his chair and put his cigarette out. Eddie watched him. "So, how about that cigarette?" he asked.

"Alright," Walter said hesitantly. He took a cigarette from his pack and stuck it into Eddie's mouth. He flicked the lighter a few times until it lit with a bright orange and yellow flame. Eddie took an extra deep drag and blew it out.

"Thank you," Eddie said with the cigarette sticking out of his lips. "Now where was I? That's right. We both came up with different ways of delivering the toxin to the bloodstream as quickly and as effectively as possible. Neil's was a gas that attacked the respiratory system, and it worked well. Mine had to be administered via injection. Mine works quicker, but requires the user to be in close quarters. C.A.N.D.L. would have picked his method of disbursement because of how easy it is to gas an entire population."

"Are you trying to tell me that you killed Neil Darden because you were jealous of the toxin he made?" Walter asked loudly.

"No, hell no. I wasn't jealous," Eddie said defensively. He took another intoxicating drag from the cigarette sticking out of his mouth. "Neil betrayed us."

"What do you mean?' Walter asked.

"He was going to sell the toxin and delivery method to another company," Eddie reveled, blowing out his smoke. Walter then knew the answer that had been on his mind for days. The haunting question, why.

"So you killed him?" Walter said.

"They told me he was an essential part of the problem, and an essential part of the plan," Eddie replied.

"Who? What plan?" Walter asked confused.

"The higher-ups at C.A.N.D.L.. They said that he needed to be taken out for his treachery,' he answered. "We also needed a living human subject to test the toxin on. So, it was like killing two birds with one stone."

"But it wasn't as easy as you thought, was it?' Walter asked, prodding further into Eddie's mind.

"It was with Neil," he replied. "Marcia on the other hand, did not go quietly." His eyes began to swell with tears. "I didn't want to do this to her, or Thomas."

"What about me? You tried to kill me," Walter reminded him.

"I know," he whispered. "But it was made very clear to me what was going to be done if I didn't clean up the mess that I made. So I did what I needed to do."

"And because of that, you are going away for a long time," Walter said. He stood from his chair and knocked briskly on the cold steel door. Walter heard the sound of locks being unlatched and then the door swung open. As he stepped outside he was greeted by the same entourage, including Frank Barlow. They all started clapping as soon as the giant door began to close. Walter started smiling, and he meant it too. The feeling of catching the suspect and bringing justice to the case was a great satisfaction for Walter.

"That was quite impressive Pierce," Frank said smiling from ear to ear. "I have half a mind to drag you back onto the force."

"Let's not talk about your half-mind," Walter joked. A few scattered laughs sparked out amongst the group. "Did you hear what he said about C.A.N.D.L.? We need to get the ball rolling on them before they disappear."

"I need to talk to you about that," Frank said seriously.

"What about?" Walter said, stunned by Frank's sudden change of attitude.

"Well, the F.B.I. are going to be taking over on the C.A.N.D.L. part of the case," Frank answered.

"Wait, what are you talking about?" Walter asked.

"We still get Eddie, and all the credit of the case. They are just taking over the C.A.N.D.L. aspect of the case," Frank replied.

"This is bullshit and you know it," Walter yelled.

"Look, there is nothing you can do about it. Why don't you head home and get some rest. I'll call you tomorrow when the test results come in on the cigarettes butts," Frank said. "Good job Walter, I mean it." A proud look came over Frank's face that Walter had never seen before.

"Yeah, I guess you're right," Walter said. He shook Frank's hand and started walking away from the small group that had surrounded Frank and him. The hot sting of justice was still imprinted deep within his mind and body. He was glad that the case was over now. He felt good. For once in a long time, he felt really good.

Derek E. Keeling
The Umbras

Chapter 11

Black Umbras

Derek E. Keeling
The Umbras

The Umbras

Walter snuffed out his smoldering cigarette in the metal ashtray on his desk. Its embers scattered around like miniature fireworks within the ashtray. A single plume of smoke wafted up into the air. He fanned his hands through the air as fast as he could trying to spread the foul stench. After he thoroughly dispersed it throughout the room, he picked up a stack of papers. His eyes scanned them visually, but his mind did not take the information in. He felt like a zombie. He threw the stack of papers back onto his desk and started fidgeting with his fingers.

He started to become anxious. It had been a week since the incident with Eddie, and he was starting to get bored with sitting around and waiting for a new case to come in. After finding out that the cigarette butts at C.A.N.D.L. were a match with the cigarettes butt at the warehouse, Walter knew for sure that Eddie would be going away for a very long time. He just had to wait for the court case, which he hated. He never could understand why it took so long to go to court, especially when there was blatantly obvious evidence proving guilt. It drove him nuts. On top of all that, he needed to make money to keep his office open and food on the table. The cases were not rolling in. The money he received from Marcia was just about completely used up. He felt as if being bored and waiting for a case to walk through the door was all that he was doing. In retrospect, he was slightly glad that his services were not needed. It showed that there was less crime on the streets. But still, he had a business to run, and the lack of cases was eating at his bill and food money.

The phone cried out loudly in the small office. Walter sat up in his chair and let it ring out a couple more times, staring at the phone intently. He hoped this was the call he had been waiting for. His hand gripped the phone and picked it up from its receiver. "Detective Walter Pierce. How may I help you?" he asked politely.

"Walter, its Frank. I need you to come down to the station. We have a problem," Frank said seriously.

"Why? What's the problem?" Walter asked. A million things ran through his mind all at once.

"Just get down here," Frank replied. He sounded just as serious as he did drunk. Walter knew that Frank only drank heavily when something bad happened.

The Umbras

"Alright, I'm on my way," Walter said. He heard Frank start talking incoherently as he went to hang up the phone. It was a slur of drunken gibberish that faded out until the phone made a click noise. Walter sat in bewilderment, amazed at the sudden call from Frank. He wondered what could possibly be wrong. He drew up no conclusions. Regardless, he stood from his chair and headed to his small, but faithful, loaner car.

He arrived at the F.C.P.D. with haste. The mystery and wonder was starting to overwhelm him. He had no idea what was in store for him, and he wasn't enjoying it. Just based on the sound of Frank's voice on the phone, he knew something was askew. This was reassured by the fact that when he walked toward Frank's office, a huge gathering of suited government agents stood in and around the room. Walter slipped passed a couple agents without having any odd looks thrown his way. Frank was busy talking to a tall, slender man in a brown suit. Walter could tell that he was the one in charge, based solely by the way he commanded the attention of Frank.

"This department will be under full

investigation," Walter heard the man yell at Frank.

"We had nothing to do with this," Frank yelled back.

"That's the problem Detective," the man said. "You didn't have anything to do with this. If you would have, this wouldn't have happened." Walter threw his arm into the air and waved it like a middle school student, trying to signal the attention of Frank. Frank looked at him and gave him a surprised look.

"Alright men, I got work to do," Frank said to the agents in the room in a rude manner. The man in brown sneered at Frank and turned around.

"Let's go," he said. The agents started to file out of the room, each glancing oddly at Walter as they passed by him. As the door shut, leaving just Walter and Frank in the room, Walter sat down in the chair in front of Frank's desk.

"What was that all about?" Walter asked curiously. Frank grunted quietly as he stood from his chair and headed toward his small mini-bar. The gurgling of fine whiskey as it was poured into a nice rocks glass reverberated throughout the room. Frank filled the glass to the brim and took a big drink. A sour look came over his face as he swallowed the potent alcohol. It was followed by a very dry exhaling of air. He walked back to his chair and sat down. He gave Walter a long and penetrating stare. Walter began to feel a little uneasy by Frank's display of incongruity.

"Eddie's dead," Frank exclaimed suddenly. Walter sat up in his chair and a concerned look came over his face.

"What? How?" Walter asked surprised.

"He was found dead in his cell early this morning," Frank replied.

"What happened to him?" Walter said.

"We're not completely sure," Frank answered hesitantly.

"What do you mean?" Walter prodded.

"Well, it's kind of unusual," Frank said slowly. "He was found dead in his cell with the same needle mark that he gave Neil Darden."

"You mean a needle mark on the back of the neck?" Walter asked.

"Yeah," Frank answered. "No one was seen going to, at, or leaving the crime scene around the time of death. It's a little baffling to be honest."

"So you don't have any suspects?" Walter said.

"No, everyone is kind of stumped at this point," Frank replied.

"I'd look into the C.A.N.D.L employees. I bet they're behind this," Walter said. "With everything that Eddie has told us, I'd say that they're trying to cover their tracks." A drunken grin peeled itself across Frank's face.

"That's actually another one of our problems," Frank said laughing, followed by taking another sip of his drink.

"What do you mean?" Walter asked confused at the statement.

"Besides Eddie being found dead, one of the reasons the F.B.I. were here, is because the C.A.N.D.L. building was burned to the ground. No survivors were found, all presumed dead," Frank said. Walter placed his hands over his face in disgust, and in confusion.

"Why?" Walter said rhetorically. His mind paced back and forth in his head searching for a reason why this would have happened. Silence turned the room cold for a moment.

Walter could feel the chills run up his

back as he thought of The Umbras. He slowly began to attempt to piece it together in his mind. All of the things he learned in his investigation began to swarm his brain, trying desperately to align themselves into a recognizable form. The Umbras were something Walter was trying to forget, but it seemed to make sense. Allen Black had told him that The Umbras toxin was supposedly untraceable, and that the C.A.N.D.L.'s toxin was not. So he took a shot in the dark. "Did you run a toxicology test on Eddie?" Walter asked, breaking the stiff silence.

"Yeah we did. Well, the F.B.I. had their men do the test, but they did it in our lab," Frank answered.

"What'd you find?" Walter asked.

"Nothing," Frank said, confirming Walter's fears.

"Nothing?" Walter reiterated.

"Yeah, nothing," Frank repeated defensively. "That and the building burning down is why we've ruled C.A.N.D.L. out as suspects."

"I agree," Walter said. "I don't think they had anything to do with this."

"Then who do you think it was?" Frank

asked. Walter didn't reply, he just sat in his chair staring at the table, thinking intently about what he was about to say.

"The Umbras," he answered.

"Oh, this again. They don't exist Pierce," Frank said.

"No, think about it. The Umbras find out about C.A.N.D.L. and what they are doing with this toxin that rivals theirs," Walter pointed out. "So, they take out the competition. From what I've gathered they are famous for taking out their competitors, so to speak."

"And who have you gathered information this from?" Frank asked with a unconvinced smirk. "Allen Black?"

"Yeah, but I'd say it's at least worth checking out. Don't you think?" Walter asked

"No, I think its outlandish. A bunch of stupid conspiracy theories," Frank replied. "And plus, the F.B.I. has full control of this investigation. We have no more jurisdiction when it pertains to this case, period."

"I can't believe you're going to just sit back and let the F.B.I. take this over," Walter stated.

"Listen, the F.B.I. told me that many

higher-ups are looking into this, and that the involvement of the F.C.P.D., or any other local branch of enforcement agency would not be needed. This means you Walter, just as much as it means me," Frank said.

"I still don't think it's right Frank," Walter said. He stood from his chair and headed for the door. He was not happy with all of the news he received. The entirety of the situation was an onslaught of his integrity. He felt used, and useless.

"Hey, I don't want you running around the city having any more to do with this case, okay? It's not only your ass if you do, it's mine too," Frank said standing from his chair.

"I can't make any promises," Walter said cracking a smile as he opened the door to Frank's office. Frank sloppily sat back down in his chair without replying. Walter could see him taking another long drink from his glass as he closed the door to the office.

He sat in the little loaner car stunned. He was thoroughly angered at the current state of things. But he knew if he did anything about it, he would lose his business, or even be put away in prison for a long time for interfering with a government agency. At the same time, he didn't care. Justice was important to him, he wasn't sure why, but it was. And he knew that justice was not being served.

He turned the car on and put it into drive. As he pulled out of the parking lot, he looked in his rear-view mirror. He noticed a black van start up that was parked on the side of the road. It slowly pulled up behind Walter's little loaner car as he stopped at the traffic light. It's headlights were turned off and the windows were tinted as dark as night.

He took a right-hand turn, and then a left-hand turn, trying to see if the van would follow. It did, with flawless accuracy. It stayed closely behind him, but it did not try to ram him or chase him down, it just followed him. Walter wondered what their intentions were. He took another left-hand turn and sped up a little, testing the van. Suddenly, the van's headlights turned on, blinding Walter for a moment. He could hear the sound of the van's engine roaring as the driver of the van stepped on the gas.

"Here we go…," Walter muttered as he slammed his right foot onto the gas pedal. The cars sped away, disappearing into the thick Francis City fog.

Derek E. Keeling
The Umbras

© *Shad Hamilton*

Derek E. Keeling is a writer and musician that lives and works in Portland, Oregon. He is also the Co-C.E.O. of the prestigious production company, *SouthEast Productions* (S.E.P.).

If you would like to get in contact with Derek E. Keeling, please email or visit his blog.

Email: dareric1@yahoo.com

Blog: http://derekkeeling.blogspot.com